*The*
# River Ghost

**Also by**
# Thomas D. Clagett

*Blood West*

*Line of Glory*

*West of Penance*

*The Pursuit of Murieta*

# *The*
# River Ghost

## A Gothic Western

## Thomas D. Clagett

RIO LOBO PRESS
Santa Fe, New Mexico, U.S.A.

Print: ISBN 978-1-953405-08-1
eBook: ISBN 9781-953405-09-8

LCCN: 2025918182

Book design: Eddie Vincent, ENC Graphic Services
Cover design by ENC Graphic Services
Cover photographs © Shutterstock

RIO LOBO PRESS

Santa Fe, New Mexico, U.S.A.

*For Janet St. Amant, my wonderful friend*

# Chapter One

For all the ghostly tales I told my girls, I never thought I would live one.

To begin, my name is Catherine Danaher. I was born and raised in the city of Pittsburgh in Western Pennsylvania and, for reasons I shall explain later, I joined the Order of the Sisters of Mercy there in January of 1883. My first two years would be spent as a postulant followed by two more years devotion as a novice and then, if I was convinced my calling to be a sister was genuine, I would take my Final Vows after three more years. As a postulant my religious habit consisted of simple garments, namely a long plain black dress, a white collar and a veil of black gauze.

We were not a cloistered Order. The sisters were well-known, often seen moving up and down the streets and alleyways dispensing food, clothing, and care to the sick and poor of the city. A person's race, condition, or religious persuasion was of no consequence to us. Our religious duties also included teaching young minds reading, composition, history, geography, and the domestic sciences. Some of us served as matrons at St. Paul's Orphan Asylum for Girls, and others as nurses at Mercy Hospital with its three hundred beds over on Stevenson Street. All these responsibilities were given in due time to each of us, to see where we might best benefit the Order.

As my first service, the Mother Superior assigned me to St. Paul's

Orphan Asylum. It stood on Webster Street, next to our convent, for the buildings were joined together. Most of our charges at St. Paul's were foundlings or girls born to unwed mothers who could not care for them. Some of those orphans were angels, but there were a few urchins. Of the ninety-three orphans we had at that time, thirty of them were placed in my charge. They lived on the second floor in a long dormitory room with gray painted walls.

I had faithfully served nine months and three days as a postulant in the Order when, on that particular evening, I chose to tell my girls of the wail of the banshee. They had heard my stories of vengeful Irish ghosts and fairy-born changelings and spell-casting witches, but not this one. My Father told it to me when I was about the age of nine, the same age as some of the girls in my charge. I so enjoyed Father's scary stories, the banshee's wail being one of my favorites.

Stories from the Bible, like Noah saving the animals marching them two by two into the ark, or Aesop's fairy tales with their wily foxes, lazy hares and steady tortoises, were often asked for. But on occasion a few of the girls begged and pleaded for me to tell one of my ghastly tales of horror and dread before having to say their nightly prayers. I could not bring myself to refuse. Of course, I'd been warned not to tell such frightening stories to them before bedtime, but the poor dears loved being scared, even the ones who covered their ears with their hands as I began the telling. Before long, they, too, sat in rapt attention with eyes wide in anticipation and hands fearfully clasped over their mouths, heedful to my every word.

I turned low the bright flames of the gas lamps suspended from the ceiling until their flickering dance cast a soft yellow glow over the proceedings.

Taking the chair near the doorway, I looked about the room at my young charges. They sat up in their beds, a row of fifteen to each side.

The youngest girl was eight years old, the oldest thirteen.

Seeing their clean, scrubbed, expectant faces ready to be scared, I knew the moment had come to break the silence that enveloped the room.

"On the green sylvan land that is Ireland, nestled between the River Shannon and the gentle hills of Clare, sat the town of Clonlara," I began. "Many fine families and other decent folk called it home. But there also lived there Miss Margaret Harrigan, a spinster lady, with a back as stiff as an iron rod, a heart as shriveled as a sour apple, and on her face a scowl etched so deep it was said she was born with it.

"Miss Harrigan owned a number of properties around County Clare and on the first of every month she went about to collect the rents. With a whip in one hand and the reins in the other, she drove a worn decrepit buggy hitched to an old plow horse. She started out no later than nine o'clock in the morning and finished before the sun began to set in the late afternoon.

"That rent money was the one true joy in her life. It was well observed that the first day of the month was the only day she was ever seen with a smile on her face, or what passed for a smile for Miss Harrigan. While most folks would dance merrily to the playing of the fiddle and flute, the only music she cared for was the sound of the clinking of those coins in her purse.

"Some months her tenants were a bit short on the rent money, times often being difficult what with more babies to feed, mills shutting down and harvests suffering, and they would beg her for just a few more days. Miss Harrigan would kindly agree, and then on her return, charge the poor tenants extra for making her have to wait, as well as the time and trouble it cost her having to return.

"As she made her rounds on the first day of a late autumn month, dark and forbidding clouds gathered. Not wanting to get caught in a rainstorm, Miss Harrigan put the whip to her old horse to hurry it along. The thought of waiting a day for the storm to pass never even occurred to her. Having her money was all that mattered.

"Snatching the coins from the last of her renters, she dropped them into her purse, tied it firmly to her belt, and hurried on her way back home. The storm threatened. Winds shook the trees. The horizon grew dim. She lighted the lantern on her buggy and thought to herself, quickly now, I must get home with my money so I can count it.

"Thunder rolled with sudden loud claps. Lightning flashed, cutting stark jagged lines across the black sky. Rain poured down, sheets of it, nearly blinding in its ferocity. So hard it came it struck the ground, splashed back up and came down again.

"But on Miss Harrigan went, whipping her poor tired horse, shouting at it to go faster."

One of my girls cried out, "Oh, no!"

"In a burst of white light," I said, "a bolt of lightning struck a large birch tree. Flame and smoke rose, and the great tree fell with a mighty groan, blocking the road.

"The old horse reared. Miss Harrigan laid her whip across his back, but it would go no further, frightened it was. Determined, Miss Harrigan stood up in the buggy and, with a bellow and the lash, urged the old horse forward. And in that instant, the horse did so in an unexpected rush that threw Miss Harrigan from the buggy. She landed hard in the muddy road, her whip having flown from her hand. Sitting up, she watched as her horse, with buggy in tow, galloped away, disappearing from sight in the pelting rain.

"Drenched to the skin and her clothes bespattered with mud, Miss Harrigan angrily got to her feet, that eternal scowl on her face deepening by the moment. Making certain her purse was still tied tightly to her belt, she began the long walk home. No rain would stop her this night, or flashing lightning, or peals of thunder.

"She had not gone far when the rain halted almost as quickly as it had begun. Her shoes made squishing sounds in the mud as she followed the road, her ire rising with every determined step.

"Passing a rocky outcrop, she thought she heard a strange sound, like a baleful whimper. Slowing her pace she listened. The sound had ceased, and she decided it had been nothing after all. A few more steps she took and behind her there rose a terrifying and blood chilling howl."

Some of my girls gasped and clutched their pillows tightly in front of them.

"Miss Harrigan's legs stopped in mid-stride. Slowly she looked back over her shoulder and saw a shape leap up from behind a boulder and squat low on top of it. It let out a screeching howl. The thing had an appearance like a woman yet was not human. The face was that of an old crone but with a mass of flowing red hair. Her eyes shown with a hellish gleam, and her mouth, that awful black mouth, hung open filled with rotting teeth sharpened to points.

"So frightened she could not move, Miss Harrigan felt a cold shiver pass through the marrow of her bones for she knew she was in the presence of the banshee, an omen that meant death was near.

"The banshee, covered in tattered rags, raised a bony arm, and pointed a skeletal finger with its long, twisted fingernail at Miss Harrigan. She watched as the banshee rose up off the rocky mound and floated in the air, the rags it wore swirling about it as though caught in a wind. A long terrible scream burst from the banshee's mouth and Miss Harrigan realized the ugly specter was coming straight for her.

"Run! Run! she told herself. Her legs moved and she ran, too scared to look back. The scream of the banshee grew louder in her ears. Through the trees she saw a light drawing near. My horse and buggy, she thought. It's coming back for me!

"But it was not so. Thundering along the road toward her was the Death Coach pulled by six horses. Black as the plague they were. Seated atop the coach was the Dullahan, a horrible headless man dressed in a black cloak, driving the horses on, not with a whip but with the spine of a dead man.

"Miss Harrigan fell weakly to her knees, her mouth dry as Potter's well. The banshee wailed and circled her as the coach rolled to a stop before her. The horses snorted smoke from their nostrils and pawed at the sloppy wet ground. Human skulls mounted on either side of the coach held burning candles. The spokes of the wheels were fashioned from thighbones. A black coffin was strapped to the roof of the coach. Miss Harrigan knew well the Death Coach only appeared to take the unfortunate to the underworld, and once it begins its journey, it can never return to the underworld without a body. The banshee announced death. The Dullahan and the Death Coach brought it.

"Quaking, she lifted her eyes at the Dullahan. It reached down and picked up an object there on the seat next to it. A head! The Dullahan's own head. Its black beady eyes stared at Miss Harrigan and its mouth widened into a ghastly grin. The smell of moldy cheese assaulted her nose. That was the smell of the Dullahan's head!

"The door of the coach swung open of its own accord revealing the blackness inside. Miss Harrigan tried to scream but no sound came forth. She felt the banshee's bony hands lift her up and shove her hard inside the coach. The door slammed shut behind her with a grim finality.

"Panicked, Miss Harrigan tried to climb out through the door window, but it was too small allowing only enough room to get her head and an arm through. Turning her head, she saw the Dullahan raise his black-gloved hand and with an expert flick of his wrist snap the bony spine in the air. The crack sounded like a thunderclap. The six black horses reared and bolted down the road.

"Inside the coach, with her hands clenched into tiny fists pressed hard against her mouth, Miss Harrigan watched out the window, fear white around her eyes. Trees rushed by, faster and faster as the Dullahan urged the horses on, the sound of the spine cracking louder and louder. The coach rocked and jerked, jolting her from side to side. Mud flew from the coach wheels as it raced over the wet, peaty ground. She shut her eyes, certain the coach would crash.

"But the awful jerking ceased and with great trepidation, she opened her eyes. Out the door window, she saw the trees along the roadside getting lower and lower, and then only the tops of the trees could she see. The coach had left the muddy ground and taken flight into the night sky!

"Throwing a frightened look out the window on the other side, she saw the hideous banshee, its mouth open wide. It turned its face toward her, those hellish eyes gleaming, and emitted a scream so horrifying it shook Miss Harrigan to her very soul.

"She fell back onto the rough seat inside the coach. Death had surely come for her, but she did not want to go. Not yet, not now, not ever! The coach rose higher and higher into the black sky. She had to find a way out. The doors on either side of the coach offered the only hope of escape. With both hands she took hold of the handle of the door on the side opposite from where the banshee flew and with all the might she could summon, gave it a hard push. To her amazement, the door flew open and in that instant, she leapt out of the flying coach."

Gasps erupted around the room.

"Miss Harrigan plummeted toward the earth, and as she did, she watched the banshee and the Death Coach fly away into the night. Clutching for her purse she realized to her great horror it was not there. It must have come loose from her belt. Her money was still inside the Death Coach! And, still falling, she clawed at the empty air after it.

"The following morning, searchers found Miss Harrigan not a quarter mile from her home. She was hanging from a birch tree, her neck broken and wedged tightly into the fork of a thick branch. They said her head was cocked at the oddest of angles, her mouth open wide, and her tongue black and protruding."

A high-pitched squeal from each of my girls followed, but their squeamish cry quickly dissolved into the laugher of delight.

It was much the same with my older sister Brigid and I when my Father would tell us his scary stories at bedtime when we were children. He enjoyed the telling as much as we relished the listening and the laughing afterward. This story was a favorite for each of us, this ghostly tale, this Irish tale. And Father would remind us that it was only a coincidence that the woman in the telling was named Miss Margaret Harrigan, for it by no means had escaped Brigid's and my attention that Margaret Harrigan happened to be the name of our skinflint landlady.

"Quiet down now, girls," I said.

"But I have a question," one of my girls said. Her name was Eleanor. She was ten years old with curly hair, and freckles covering her face.

"Yes, Eleanor," I said, giving her my attention.

She tilted her head to one side and said, "If Miss Harrigan was being taken to the underworld, why did the coach fly up into the air?"

Eleanor was a most inquisitive child. It would not have surprised me if she were to become an attorney at law one day. And I should point out, in all the times Father had told this story or any of his others, I had never questioned the workings of banshees and Irish ghosts and the like. But, as I quickly tried to conceive an explanation, one of the other children, Martha, a year older than Eleanor, rolled her eyes and said, "Because the underworld is underneath the world, silly."

That produced a scattering of giggles around the room.

"All right," Eleanor said undeterred, "if the coach is not supposed to go back empty, who did the Dullahan get to take Miss Harrigan's place?"

She was looking directly at me. Glancing about, I noticed all the girls facing in my direction, expectant looks upon their faces. I had never asked Father about that one, either.

"Time for your prayers then," I said. "Out of bed, on your knees, hands together, thumbs crossed."

I heard the heavy thumps of Sister Agatha's shoes echoing down the wide hallway outside the room as she approached. Sister Agatha told me she purposely made the noise so that any mischief-makers had the chance to mend their ways before she appeared. Scolding was not in her nature, she said. However, it was odd that she was coming this way at such an hour as I thought her duties this evening consisted of preparing the children's school lessons for the coming week.

Kneeling at their bedsides, the girls recited their evening prayers, asking the good Lord to watch over them and to keep each of us safe.

The world can be a hard place, my Mother would say. There's good and evil in it. But children endure. They must.

The thumping in the hallway stopped. I knew Sister Agatha was standing outside the doorway, waiting patiently.

"Amen," the girls said as they finished their prayers and climbed into their beds.

I wished them good night as I turned down the flames of the gas lamps, and they answered telling me good night. Stepping into the hallway, I saw Sister Agatha, her face usually a pleasant round sphere framed by the white coif and black veil of the Order. Something troubled her this night.

"Mother Superior wishes to see you," she said, fingering the wooden beads of the long rosary that hung from her belt. "She says you should come right away. To her office."

Had one of the other sisters on this floor gone to Mother Superior and told her I was telling ghost stories again? Perhaps so, but a scolding could wait until morning. That was when I had received scoldings before, along with a penance of washing floors or scrubbing pots every day for a week. Entering the Order required taking vows of poverty, chastity and obedience. The latter proved particularly troublesome for me from time to time. But being summoned to Mother Superior's office at night and with that insistence to come right away did not bode well.

# Chapter Two

Quietly but quickly, I made my way through the orphan asylum and into the convent. The gas lamps lighting its hallways were dimmed. My fellow sisters in Christ had already retired for the night, though I could hear the soft whispers of a few reciting their evening prayers behind their closed doors.

I descended the staircase, careful to avoid the several stairs that emitted loud tortured groans when weight was placed upon them. The postulants were always given the task of oiling those wooden steps. I had done so many times, but the offending groans persisted.

A square of light shone against the floor near the end of the narrow hallway. The door to Mother Superior's office was open. Stepping into the doorway, I saw her seated at her desk, where she looked at the small yellow piece of paper she held in her hand. She wore spectacles perched on the bridge of her crooked nose. She had joined the Order over twenty years ago.

"You sent for me, Mother?" I asked keeping my voice low.

The hint of a sad smile crossed her face as she told me to come in and close the door. A simple curtain covered the window behind her desk. A wooden crucifix hung on the wall to the right. On the opposite wall was a schoolhouse pendulum clock, its soft tick-tock counting time.

She asked me to sit as she came around to face me. She walked with a pronounced limp, the result of a childhood injury.

"I have received very sad news, Catherine," she said and took the yellow paper from her desk. "This telegram arrived this evening. It is from your brother-in-law Charles. Your sister has died. I am so sorry."

Brigid? Dead? How? What could have happened? Good Lord, I had not seen her in almost twelve years. She had run away long ago with Charles but what had—? I realized Mother Superior was speaking to me.

"Forgive me, Mother," I said. "I didn't hear you."

"No, I understand. It's a terrible shock." She held the telegram out to me. "There's more. Do you wish to read it?"

I glanced at the clock on the wall. The pendulum continued its measured swing. Tick-tock. Steady and true. Somehow it felt oddly consoling at that moment.

I shook my head. "Please, would you tell me what it says? Does he say what she died of?"

"He doesn't mention it," she said, adjusting her spectacles. "He says, 'Imperative you come at once to offer comfort and guidance to the children until arrangements can be made for a proper governess.'"

Brigid's children? I did not even know she had children. How many were there? Charles and my sister lived far away in a place called the Territory of New Mexico. Why does he insist I come? I understood the family obligation. She was my sister. But are there no governesses there? My responsibilities were here.

"You must go, Catherine," Mother Superior said gently.

"But how can I, Mother?" I said. "My work is here. God's work is here. The orphan asylum —"

"Will still be here when you return," she said, cutting me off.

"But I've devoted my life to the Order," I said. "I can't leave. My children need me."

12

"Your sister's children need you more. And when it's time for you to return to us, you may continue with your duties."

"Yes, I, I know that," I said, "but I'm making such progress with my girls. Little Clara loves to read now. And Martha is making wonderful strides. Oh, and Eleanor. If you could only hear her."

"Catherine, stop."

I felt Mother Superior's hand on mine. Looking into her face, I saw her genuine concern.

"You are one of the most devoted postulants I have ever known," she said. "But you are also one of the most willful. That can be a gift in dealing with the poor unfortunate waifs left in our charge. But when that willfulness turns to argument, it becomes a detriment."

"I'm sorry. Please forgive me."

"Of course," she said. "This is all very upsetting. We cannot always know God's purpose, but we must be guided by His wisdom and grace."

"Yes, Mother," I said obediently. But at this moment I could not understand anything of God's purpose. I never imagined I would ever have to leave this place.

Mother Superior said that my brother-in-law had made arrangements for my train travel and expenses.

Train? I had never been on a train before.

And she said something about having Sister Agatha bring me some clothes. Of course, I would need changes of clothes.

"And you will leave tomorrow morning," Mother Superior said, "before the children awake."

My heart tightened in my chest. "I cannot tell them goodbye?"

The clock abruptly stopped. I glanced up at it. No. The pendulum still swung, the ticking steady. I was certain I heard it stop.

"Goodbyes will only make things more difficult for you and them,"

Mother Superior said. "And do not tell the other sisters you are leaving. It is late. I will explain to them."

I nodded numbly.

"Again, I know how hard this must be for you," Mother Superior said, "but God will show you in His good time."

# Chapter Three

What reason did God have for taking me away from my girls, my friends, my life? It made no sense to me. God will show you in His good time, Mother Superior liked to say, especially when difficulty arose. It was not that I could not believe it. In my heart I accepted it as true. But it did not stop me from feeling somehow betrayed, that God was not being fair. Or was this the grimness of—Oh, I had to push all these thoughts away. Far away. They would only fester and rankle me more. That would not do. Think of something else. What was it Charles had written? Until arrangements can be made for a proper governess. Yes, arrangements would be made, and I would return here to the convent, to my girls. Soon. I would come back very soon.

I waited patiently in my cell. That was what our austere quarters inside the convent were called. A table, a bed, a chair and a couple of wall pegs to hang our clothes on were all our vow of poverty allowed us.

When we joined the Order, we had to give up our clothes and other worldly possessions. It was part of our promise of devotion to God and the religious life. Our things were then donated to the poor. On the day I entered the convent I had tried to hide the one possession of mine I could not bring myself to part with. It was a small silver crucifix on a delicate chain I wore around my neck. In my moment of weakness I quickly slipped it off and placed it inside my mouth next to my cheek. Two sisters escorted me to the robing room, asking me questions and I answered without difficulty or incident. Inside the robing room I gave over my clothes and put on my postulant's garments. I still had the crucifix and chain in my mouth, having had no opportunity to remove it. As I placed the veil on my head, Mother Superior entered the room. I had been instructed to bow my head to her as sign of reverence and did so. Without a word, she held out her open hand to my mouth. How had she known? Shame-faced, I allowed the crucifix and chain to fall from my mouth into her hand. She raised a disapproving eyebrow at me. I told her the crucifix and chain had been my Mother's.

There was a tentative knock at the door. It was Sister Agatha, a sad look on her face. I invited her in. She carried a simple muslin dress and a dark coat in one hand, and a straw hat and a faded carpetbag in the other. The clothes had belonged to the new postulant who had joined the Order the week before, she said. Fortunately for me her clothes had not yet been given to charity. I took them from her and laid them on my bed.

"I knew you were leaving us when Mother Superior told me to bring some clothes to you," Sister Agatha said. "One of the sisters found the carpetbag at the convent door. Someone left it there. I thought we could find a use for it, but I think you need it more."

I thanked her and before I could say another word, she said, "I'm not supposed to ask you any questions or say anything else, but I want you to know that sometimes in the evenings I would stand in the hallway and listen to the ghastly stories you told your girls. Mother Superior said they were against the rules and we should tell her when you did so. But I liked them, especially your ghost stories. I will miss—" She drew in a short breath as though the

16

words caught in her throat and smiled tightly. "I will miss them." She hurried out of my room, pulling the door closed behind her.

Sister Agatha had a good heart and a kind soul. I hated to leave her, too.

The dress she brought was in need of hemming. That new postulant stood half a foot taller than me. The instruction my Mother had given to me years before showing me how to whip stitch came in quite handily that night. Putting the straw hat on my head I thought it fit and would suffice. We had no mirrors in the convent for they might induce vanity.

I found the coat a little roomy when I tried it on, but with winter coming I was glad to have it. Removing it, I noticed the end of a red woolen scarf hanging from the pocket. I pulled it out and as I did, an item dropped from its folds onto my bed. I looked at it in disbelief for it was my Mother's silver crucifix and chain.

My knees weakened. I had to sit down, overcome I was. Had Mother Superior kept it all this time? Did she put it and the scarf in the pocket of the coat for me? How else could it be? Asking her would have to wait until my return. I fastened the chain and crucifix around my neck, vowing I would never take it off while I was on this journey.

I opened my copy of the Divine Office. Mother Superior had presented it to me the day I joined the Order. This was the book of daily prayers containing psalms and verses from the Bible every novice and postulant and sister read without fail. Sanctifying each day with prayer begins with reading our first prayer at dawn, then the morning prayer, followed by one at midmorning, midday, mid-afternoon, vespers that evening and the nightly prayer. Mother Superior told us reciting these daily prayers was important for they reminded us of our promise and devotion to Christ and the sacrifice

He made for our salvation. Turning to the prayer for this night I read, but my distractions confounded my concentration. The last line I read was from the Psalms and I could go no further. *I raise my eyes toward the mountians, From whence shall come my help? My help comes from the Lord, the maker of heavan and earth.*

Later, I lay awake in my bed in the dark, my thoughts and feelings raw and jumbled. Too many things had happened this night, too many sad and terrible things. I humbly asked God to watch over me and pulled the covers close.

# Chapter Four

My journey began early the next morning under a slate-colored sky. I remember the date. September 20. It was a Saturday.

I opened the Divine Office. The first prayer was from the Psalms. *Graciously rescue me, God! Come quickly to help me, Lord!* When I finished the reading, I brought Mother's silver crucifix to my lips, kissed it then slipped it down inside the front of my borrowed dress. It would not do to have it accidently catch on something and get torn off. Neatly folding my postulant's dress, I placed it on my pillow, and on top of it, my white collar and black veil. I buttoned my coat and quietly left the brick confines of the convent for the train depot. The train was scheduled to depart at six o'clock.

The morning was cool, though the air felt thicker and more humid than usual. Passing the orphan asylum, I dared not look up, as Eleanor or Martha or some of my other girls might already be awake and peering down from the window of their room to find me walking away, a straw hat on my head and a carpetbag clutched in my hand. The sight of their innocent questioning faces would be more than I could bear.

My eyes welled with tears. No time to dally. My feet gained speed, moving it seemed with a mind of their own. The worn heels of my simple black shoes made dull clacking sounds against the damp bricks of the street.

Rounding a corner I slowed, taking in several deep breaths and dried my eyes. The sound of a loud gurgling croak overhead drew my attention. Looking up between the buildings, I saw a large black bird, a raven, circling in the sky above me, its tail feathers sharply pointed, much like its large beak, and its dark wings spread wide. And then I heard a different cry, harsh and shrill, as another raven suddenly appeared. It swooped down on the circling one, clipping its back as though picking a fight or maybe settling a grudge. It refused to give up the attack. I could not wait around to see the outcome.

Vendors appeared on the streets. Horse-drawn delivery wagons were making their rounds. Men in blackened work clothes headed for the steel factories.

Reaching the depot, I caught my reflection in a window. The coat appeared more generous on me than I had thought now that I saw myself. I removed my hat, curious to see my face after these many months. I thought I had changed little. Except for my hair. It was the one thing I had treasured, the one thing I thought pretty about myself. The Order did require the sisters on taking their Final Vows to cut their hair off as a sign of their devotion, but postulants were under no such obligation. However, I had asked that they take the shears to my long tresses. I saw no reason to delay. A new life was awaiting me. When the deed was finished, the hair left on my head fell abruptly to the nape of my neck. I had kept it so since, without regret.

Boarding the train, I prayed for a miracle from God to prevent it from leaving. Nothing that would harm a life, mind you. A pillar of fire to block the way, or the river suddenly rising and flooding out the tracks would have done nicely. I heard the conductor call out and the train lurched slowly forward. Clouds of white steam hissed from the great locomotive. A plume of black smoke shot straight up from the funnel-shaped stack. Leaving the depot, two things were quite clear to me. First, that God intended I should go on this westward trek. And second, as I had heard my Father say on certain occasions, the Irish had used up their allotment of miracles from God.

As the train crossed the Monongahela River, I gazed out the window of the passenger car at the tall smokestacks of the steel factories, the heart of Pittsburgh. Row after row of the dark brick chimneys lined the river as far as I could see, churning out the never-ending billows of black smoke rising high into the sky. When Brigid and I were children, we fretted that the blue sky would soon be blotted out by the gloomy blackness. Mother comforted us, saying we needn't worry for the smoke would soon drift away, carried off by the winds. But there always remained what the wind failed to carry off, that ever-present sticky soot. It clung to hair and clothes, to the windows and buildings, to lampposts and sidewalks, to everything. And Father, being Father, liked to tell us that Pittsburgh was just hell with the lid off, and Mother would scold him for trying to scare us.

In spite of this picture of perdition, this place was my home, the only one I had known. And I hated to leave it, if only for a time. Mother was buried here. And Father. He had worked as a laborer at the Black Diamond Steel factory owned by the Park Brothers. He would come home to the three little cramped rooms we lived in on Carson Street, his clothes covered in that awful black soot and a dark oily grime caked under his fingernails. Mother would tell him to go to the sink and wash, as she would not allow dirty hands at her clean table. Father liked to say his job was a fine one, "a job of sweat and gold," he called it. And Mother would quickly add, "Aye, you do the all the sweating, and the Brothers Park get all the gold."

Though she rarely spoke of it, Mother worried that one day word would come of a terrible calamity, that Father had fallen into a vat of molten steel, or worse. That black day finally did arrive, but it was no horrible factory accident that befell Father. Walking home on that cold frosty evening, he slipped on the ice and cracked his head open when it struck the edge of a brick sidewalk. A policeman and our priest, Father Lynch, brought his body home. Mother could not stop her crying, though she tried her best to console us. Brigid was eleven. I was nine.

Soon after, Mother took a job as a scrubwoman to keep a roof over our heads and food on the table. Brigid and I said we would leave school and go to work to help bring in money. Mother was grateful for our concern, but she would not hear of it. "You cannot go ignorant in this world," she told us, "and don't let anyone try to convince you otherwise. You speak up for yourselves but there is never a need to be rude. Always tell the truth and shame the devils. Use the brains God gave you for they are a blessing." Brigid and I remained in school. While we struggled vainly with arithmetic, it was reading and composition that proved to be real joys for the both of us.

However, Brigid was blessed with something I was not. She inherited Mother's chestnut red hair and hazel green eyes, gently rounded curves and skin pale as porcelain. And by the by, that chestnut red hair of hers was so thick it could choke the teeth of a comb. As to myself, I favored Father. His hair was dark and his eyes were blue, and I shall leave it at that.

It should come as no surprise then that Brigid received more than a fair lot of attention from boys. They cajoled and coaxed, some more ardently than others, and I am pleased to say my sister was not one easily flattered.

But shortly after her seventeenth birthday, Brigid met Charles Preston. He was a few years older than her and claimed he was studying the law. Mother did not approve of him, thinking him a scoundrel.

Oh, he was handsome all right, and educated and charming. Maybe too charming. He had a twinkle in his eye, disarming and beguiling. Mother said she could see the devil in those eyes of his.

Of course, Mother's disapproval only encouraged Brigid's desire to step out with young Mr. Preston on any occasion she could find. It was not long before Brigid told Mother and me she had fallen in love with Charles and that he had asked her to be his wife. Mother forbid Brigid to marry him. That same night Brigid eloped. She left a note. We found it in the morning on the kitchen table. It said she was sorry to have run away but she had to pursue her happiness. She hoped that Mother would understand and asked for her forgiveness for going against her wishes.

We had no money to chase her, let alone bring her back. The county sheriff said she and Charles were likely out of his jurisdiction by now anyway.

"If only your Father was here," Mother said, looking at me, the hurt plain in her eyes. "He would know what to do."

About three months later we received a letter from Brigid. I read it to Mother who refused to even touch it. Brigid had married Charles and was now living in a strange sounding place called Santa Fe far out west in the Territory of New Mexico. Her husband was clerking in a law office and expected to be admitted to the bar before year's end. He would be a tremendous success, she was certain of it. At the end of the letter she wrote, I love and miss you both.

Mother stared straight ahead for a few moments, saying nothing. Then she turned to me and said, "I no longer have two daughters. I have only you."

Mother was stubborn Irish and once her mind was made up there was no changing it. In spite of our Catholic faith and love of family, in Mother's eyes, Brigid had betrayed her and me and also Father. Short of Brigid returning on her knees to beg forgiveness, there would be no reconciliation. But I knew this situation broke Mother's heart for I heard her crying in her room late that night. It was a terrible weeping. Worried, I went in to see what was the matter. Mother was sitting on her bed, her face buried in her pillow. She lifted her face and said it was nothing for me to concern myself about and to go back to sleep. In the morning she told me she was sorry she woke me and if it should happen again, I was to ignore her sobs.

I blamed Brigid for these troubles, blamed her for being so selfish. But somehow, I also understood. She always dreamed of going away to exciting places, often entertaining us with wild stories of her imaginary travels. Many a time I found her in the library looking at books about different countries in the world. Falling in love, getting married and raising a family were her real goals, though. She had gotten that from stories Father liked to tell of Ireland, of his home. But slipping away in the dark of night with a man to get married was an insult, a slap in the face. I knew well how much it hurt Mother, but it stung me, too, for Brigid and I had always been very close. I hoped she could have trusted me enough to tell me of her plans. Perhaps I might have softened the blow on Mother. My deep resentment soon faded and I came to the realization that Brigid was fulfilling her dreams. For that I was happy, though I did not care for her choice of husband.

About six months later Mother took a terrible fall down a staircase she was scrubbing. "T'was a miracle I didn't break my fool neck," she said. Bedridden, she could no longer work and needed my constant care. Having finished my schooling the year before, I had taken a job stitching clothing. Being from a poor Irish family it was either that or assembling artificial flowers. But now I had to quit to care for Mother. I was the one to have to feed and bathe her, change her bedding, and dress her daily. Without telling her, I wrote to my sister, as I believed she should know what had happened. Not long after, a check arrived from Brigid. No letter, no explanation. The amount was more than enough to cover our rent, food and anything else we needed.

At first Mother told me to send the check back with a stern note that we had no need for any consideration from "the likes of her." Mother was a proud woman. She wanted nothing to do with that "guilt money" as she called it. "But we need the money," I said. "Bills are due, and food is not appearing like manna from heaven." It galled Mother, but she did finally accept that it was necessary to take the money.

I wrote Brigid, thanking her. As I mentioned earlier, I held no ill feelings for Brigid. I was happy for her, and told her so in my letter, adding that I also wished she had not run away in the night without so much as a goodbye. She wrote back how very sorry she was about the way she had left. We are sisters, she said. Nothing can change our blood. She also mentioned little of her husband. That struck me as queer. I tried not to let it worry me, but it did weigh on my mind. Had Charles's plans somehow soured? Were he and Brigid still happy? I thought perhaps a letter to her from Mother might bring a more revealing response and so I asked Mother if she would like me to write to Brigid for her. She drew her mouth into a thin line and shook her head.

The checks continued to arrive, one every month. And once in a while, a letter came. Brigid still would not say much about her husband but did mention he was now a member of the bar and that his law practice was thriving. Santa Fe, she said, was a frontier town, not at all like Pittsburgh, but she added nothing more. Something still felt terribly wrong to me, and I worried about my sister's happiness. I wrote to her of my concerns. My entreaties went unanswered.

Caring for Mother included reading stories to her. Every Sunday I read to her from the Bible. She insisted, being unable to attend Mass. She never lost her faith in God, praying every day. "God will take care of us," she would say. "God will see us through." Other days she enjoyed hearing *David Copperfield, A Tale of Two Cities, A Christmas Carol,* and other books by Mr. Charles Dickens. She had no interest in French stories about bell-ringing hunchbacks or silly musketeers, nor the "female tales" as she called them of Jane Austen. "Those women wouldn't last a day digging in the peat bogs of Ireland," she said with distain. Now and again, she would ask me to tell one of Father's Irish ghost stories. It was her way of remembering him, I think. I know she missed him. I did, too. I missed Brigid. I missed our lives together.

Brigid had been away nine years when Mother took very ill that winter. A terrible winter it was, too. The doctor said she had developed pneumonia. I wrote to Brigid asking her to please come home. Before I received any response, Mother's conditioned suddenly worsened. Pleurisy, the doctor called it. Mother could barely speak. Her breathing sounded like a struggle of wet rasps and gurgles.

A letter arrived about a week later from Brigid saying she wanted to come but that she had taken ill herself and would travel as soon as she recovered. That night as Mother lay in her bed, shivering under her blankets, she motioned to me. I bent down close to her and she said in a ragged whisper, "Tell Brigid I love her."

Mother died the following morning. She was buried on a Wednesday. It was a gray morning. A light snow fell. I watched as the delicate white flakes settled on her coffin. I thought of them as angels' kisses. Father Lynch gave the service. I wished I could have had flowers to place on her grave.

I mailed Brigid a letter that afternoon telling her that Mother was at peace now and would suffer no more. I included what Mother had told me to tell her.

Brigid wrote back. Her words were full of sadness and heartbreak, but she also said her heart was mending with the sweetness of Mother's loving message. If there was anything she could do for me, I should let her know.

That evening, I composed a long letter telling her I was joining the Sisters of Mercy. The Mother Superior at the convent had been most inviting. You see, I could not depend on the kindnesses of my sister forever. I told Brigid she no longer needed to send the much-appreciated checks. I would very shortly be in the tender care of the sisters.

Mother had discussed my future with me after her accident. She said I had intelligent eyes and a sharp mind, but I was as plain as paper. Sewing men's trousers and ladies' dresses was a drudgery I did not deserve. A sister's life would suit me best. "You have caring hands and a strong constitution," she told me. "The sisters will see that. They'll know St. Paul's will be the place for you. The orphans will be your children, your happiness."

I came to accept that Mother was right. There had been no suitors knocking at the door. Ever. Changes had come over me, in body and mind and soul. Sweet changes, and others mysterious.

On the day I entered the dormitory room at St. Paul's and saw the faces of the girls entrusted to my care, I recalled Mother's words. "The orphans will be your children, your happiness." I wanted to help and care for these orphans. I knew I would never have children of my own. Only the orphans.

# Chapter Five

"Ticket, please," a wheezy voice said.

Glancing up from my seat by the window, I saw the portly conductor holding his ticket punch in his thick fingers. He wore a blue uniform with a black bow tie, a shiny badge on his cap and a gold watch chain stretching across his stomach from one vest pocket to the other. Taking my ticket from my carpetbag, I handed it to him and asked if he could tell me how far it was to Santa Fe.

"New Mexico Territory?" he said, punching the ticket and cocking his head to one side, as if calculating in the air above him. "Close to two thousand miles, little lady. You have a long trip ahead of you." He handed my ticket back to me, tipped his cap and moved on.

Two thousand miles! I could hardly imagine such a distance. What was this West that I was headed for? As a youngster I had heard Father talking about the nefarious James brothers, Jesse and Frank, well known for their many bank robberies. More recently there were stories from the newspaper I was familiar with. A marshal named Wyatt Earp and his brothers in the Arizona Territory had battled a gang of miscreants in a town called Tombstone. Tombstone! What kind of name is that for a town? A thief and murderer named Billy the Kid had been slain in this New Mexico Territory. It was said that others like him and worse still roamed there. And there were the strange names I had heard, like Crazy Horse and Shotgun Johnny Collins and Wild Bill Hickock.

I refused to give in to panic. Fear would not rule me. I had Brigid's children to think of. These youngsters were soon to become my responsibility. And yet they were complete strangers to me. And what of Brigid? How had she died? What were the circumstances? I wanted and needed answers.

*       *       *

We rolled through the forested hills of eastern Ohio. The first hints of yellow gold tainted the leaves signaling the approach of autumn. The gentle rocking of the train and the steady click-clack of its wheels on the rails became a kind of comfort.

I counted close to two dozen other passengers in the car with me. Nearly every seat was taken. Sitting across the aisle from me was a young couple. He kept a protective arm around his wife who was expecting a child, and was so well along, I thought she might have it at any moment. I saw only two other single ladies. One was traveling with her brother. I overheard that he was taking her to a sanitarium for her health. The other was an older woman, rigid in her manner and countenance. First, she demanded a window be opened for she felt the air stifling. Once it was opened, she insisted it be closed as she claimed to be smothered with dust.

Along our route we made stops at stations every thirty miles or so to take on water. At many of them was a small place called a roadhouse with tables and chairs offering quick meals. That first day I stepped off the train to allow my legs to stretch as well as to investigate one of these roadhouses. It offered a stew of potatoes and meat with a slice of bread. I was satisfied with the cheese sandwich and a sliced apple I had brought with me from the convent kitchen.

Fortunately, the passenger seats were cushioned with what the conductor said was horsehair making sleep somewhat possible, though I was unused to sleeping sitting up. I do not wish to sound as though I was ungrateful. Far from it. However, the loud snores emanating from some of the other passengers were very unsettling.

I woke early the next morning, opened the Divine Office, read my morning prayer, and kissed Mother's silver crucifix. As it was Sunday and Mass services were not available, I closed my eyes, made the sign of the cross, and prayed for thirty minutes, asking God to keep me safe on my journey and to help me with the task I had been given.

*   *   *

At St. Louis we crossed over the Mississippi River. I had grown up between the Monongahela and the Allegheny Rivers and had thought them the mightiest and most important rivers ever with their constant commerce of riverboats and barges. But the Mississippi was far grander, truly the great Father of Waters as Brigid had told me it was called, having read about it in one of her books.

Also, at St. Louis our passenger population dwindled by half, but there were those who made it a colorful collection. A man with a florid face held some of us spellbound for many miles with stories of a traveling circus he had owned before selling it to a man named Barnum. And he had a slew of stories. He told us how he smuggled serpent charmers out of India, trained Arabian horses to dance, and journeyed to the island of Fiji and brought back a real live mermaid. Entertaining he was, but I believed with each passing tale that he traded more in blarney than in truth.

Did I mention that Kansas was the flattest piece of God's good earth I had ever seen? I could not imagine a place that stretched out so blank and dismal for so long. Telegraph poles swished by endlessly, tediously. The long grasses were dried up. Not a tree or a shrub in sight. It was as though all green had been banished.

\*    \*    \*

Delays hampered us, as well. One such delay, something to do with the boiler we were told, resulted in our arriving late in Topeka, Kansas. I had already missed my scheduled train, but fortune was with me as another train was at that moment departing. Knowing full well I would have shocked my sisters in Christ with my next action, I had no choice as I was determined to catch that train. With my carpetbag in one hand, I hiked my skirt up with the other and ran like a Protestant across the wooden platform, shouting at the conductor who was standing on the open vestibule of the last car. He shouted an oath, leaned over the car railing and stretched out his hand to me. Several people stepped forward to see what all the commotion was, and I nearly knocked them over rushing by. Letting go of my skirt, I took hold the conductor's hand, and he pulled me aboard with only a few feet of platform remaining.

"That was the most foolish thing I have ever seen a woman do," the conductor scolded me. Then his pink cherub face softened, and he laughed, "And I'll never forget it long as I live. After all that, I hope you have a ticket."

# Chapter Six

Stopping that night to take on water and passengers at the town of Emporia, a long-legged fellow rushed to catch the train. Winded, he entered the car I was sitting in. He had bristly muttonchop whiskers, wore checkered trousers and carried a valise over his shoulder. Taking the seat across from me he introduced himself as Fletcher Fairchild and said he was a writer of exciting true stories of the West.

"My travels take me far and wide in search of dramatic new stories to tell," he said and smiled. "I have been published by the firm of Beadle and Adams. Eighteen books in three years. This is my latest."

Reaching into his valise, he produced a thin volume entitled, *Captured by the Comanches: The Adventures of Constance Wiley. A Story of Red Horror on the Black Mesa.* On the cover was a picture of a woman, her back against a rock wall and a terrified expression on her face as a black shadow loomed up before her.

"The cost to you," he said, "only one thin dime. A true bargain!"

So, this was one of those dime novels. Sister Agatha told me she had seen them on her rounds of Pittsburgh. These lurid tales of marauding savages and vicious outlaws were popular with adolescent boys and young men.

"It could help pass the time, miss," he said.

I gave him a brief shake of my head, said I was tired and settled back into my seat as I preferred getting some sleep rather than consorting with Constance Wiley and her troubles.

I awoke the next morning and realized we were stopped. I heard the sound of wind gusting outside. I was startled at what presented itself outside the nearby window. A dark, dusty, slow moving mass of cows spread over the flat land ahead of us. I had never seen so many of these animals at one time. Beyond it rising up in the distance stood Dodge City. It was not much more than a couple of rows of wooden buildings lining a single street.

I smoothed my dress, put on my straw hat, and found the conductor.

"What has happened?" I asked. "Why are we stopped?"

The conductor chuckled and said, "Cattle. Close to three thousand head, I'd say. May as well settle in, miss. We're going to be here for a while until the herders get them across the tracks."

"Conductor!" a woman of peevish disposition called out as she marched down the aisle, her jaw set and eyes narrowed. "I paid good money for my ticket. Why do I have to wait for these cows?"

The conductor tipped his cap. "Courtesy, ma'am. They were here first."

I brought my hand to my mouth to cover my smile as the woman made an indignant noise and walked away, grumbling.

Pulling down the window, I stuck my head out to see if I could get a better look when a gust of wind snatched my hat off my head. The wind carried it across the ground and right into the herd of cattle crossing the tracks where it disappeared amid their legs. While the hat held no special interest for me, I still felt a little foolish for having lost it, but I was also disappointed, as I had no hat now.

*   *   *

We pushed westward. Reaching Colorado proved a disappointing sight. Distant summit peaks sat draped in dreary gray clouds.

"It's a shame the Rocky Mountains are hiding from you, this being your first look at them," the conductor said to me. "But I can assure you, they are majestic. The air is so crisp up there. Like breathing champagne."

I had heard of champagne and could only imagine that mountain air must have a ticklish sensation on the lungs. But it was also in Colorado that I noted the air was thin and crisp, not at all like the thick oppressive air of Pittsburgh.

During the night we crossed into the Territory of New Mexico. Stopping at the town of Las Vegas—someone said it means "the meadows" in English—a most uncanny thing occurred. I stepped off the passenger car to take a short walk, as I often did whenever we stopped, and out in a field beyond the tracks I saw three large black birds clustered together. Ravens, they were. I recognized them, for I recalled two of their cousins had flown over me when I was walking to the train depot in Pittsburgh, one attacking the other. Peering more closely I saw these three were feeding, tearing the bloody entrails from the carcass of some unfortunate animal. Ghastly.

A shrill blast from the train whistle startled me and the ravens took flight, their great black wings making a soft whooshing sound as they did. They flew high into the clear blue sky. But one of them banked and came swooping back toward earth, making a deep croaking call, coming directly at me, its call turning to a deadly shrill cry. I crouched, ducking my head as the black shape flew over me.

The conductor came running. "Did it get you, miss? Are you hurt?"

"I'm fine," I said.

"Time to get aboard," he said, helping me up into the car. "Strange about that raven."

"You mean that it came after me?"

"You did nothing to provoke it," he said shaking his head. "Very strange."

* * *

Mountains appeared. Not like the Rocky Mountains the conductor had described to me, but some boasted great slabs of rock jutting up. And others stood long and flat as tabletops. I was told they were called *mesas*.

Scrubby plants sprouted out of the brown earth. Some were truly beautiful, and I said as much to a bearded passenger sitting across from me.

"Them's sagebrush," he said. "They won't hurt you."

"What do you mean?"

"I take it you're new to the Territory."

"Yes, I am."

"Well, you should know that out here if it crawls it's got fangs and if it grows it'll stick you."

I thought he surely must be overstating things. "But didn't you just tell me that sagebrush wouldn't hurt me?"

"You got me there, miss, but there's still truth in what I said. We got all manner of thorns and needles here. You see those green spiny-looking varmints out there?" He pointed out the window indicating odd-looking plants about three to four feet high. The branches jutted out at sharp angles that I could only describe as angry. Hundreds of them peppered the land. "You want to stay clear of those, miss."

"And why is that?" I asked.

"It's a prickly cactus," he said. He said the name and it sounded so strange. *Cholla*. "Got barbs all over them," he went on. "Eight, ten needles to a barb. They stuck me more than a few times. Tenacious they are, and vicious because they don't want to let go. Like the devil hisself grows them."

I thanked him and planned to do my best to keep away from their sting.

Then he made a clicking sound out of the corner of his mouth and said, "It's a funny thing about them cactus. They get a real pretty flower on them come springtime. Some purple, some yellow."

The conductor came through the car announcing we would be in Santa Fe in a couple of hours. It was Tuesday, the thirtieth of September. With changing trains and delays, I had traveled ten days to get here. And the questions rushed forward in my mind. What had happened to Brigid? How had she died? What of her children? I wanted answers from Charles.

Two tall mountain ranges soon came into view. One to the west was opal in color. The other, to the north, stood resplendent in red majesty with swaths of crimsons and yellows, as though painted against the mountainsides. I had no doubt, had Mr. Shakespeare seen them, he would have been inspired to compose a new sonnet.

We stopped at the depot where I would change trains for the last trek of my journey, another eighteen miles to go. A couple of men were patching holes on the slanted roof of the rough walled depot. A sign read Lamy Junction. It was as desolate a spot as I had yet seen. Rocky jagged hills surrounded it. Only two other buildings stood across the way. The John Pflueger General Merchandise store had a wooden façade. Next to it was a place made of stone blocks called the Annex Saloon. A few of my fellow passengers hastily made their way to its door. One of them was the long-legged Mr. Fairchild in his checkered pants. Even with his valise full of books, he easily outdistanced the others.

On the opposite side of the depot rose a small mountain. Reddish brown in color it bore an uncanny resemblance to a loaf of bread. Except whole sections had been cleaved out of its side for I could plainly see evidence of vertical cuts in the rocks. How very strange.

The conductor called out for passengers embarking for Santa Fe. A few minutes later we were moving backwards. Flustered by this, I turned to the passenger sitting behind me and asked him about it. The passenger, a bearded man who frowned at being interrupted while reading his newspaper, said something about it being a spur line meaning it only ran from Lamy Junction to Santa Fe. "No need for the locomotive to turn around, miss," he said gruffly and went back to his newspaper. In spite of his explanation, it still felt odd to be traveling backwards into my destination.

I opened the Divine Office and read the midday prayer.

The train chugged slowly as the grade was almost entirely uphill. Nearly two hours passed before we pulled into Santa Fe. Pittsburgh may have been black with soot and smoke, but Santa Fe lay brown as mud beneath the red mountains.

# Chapter Seven

The man who met me at the train depot introduced himself as John Jessup. His accent sounded Southern. He said Mr. Preston had sent him and he would see me to Mr. Preston's house. He offered to carry my bag. When I said it was not necessary, he kindly insisted, and we made our way along the platform crowded with passengers disembarking from the train and those meeting them.

Mr. Jessup was a gangling man of about forty. Dressed in blue jeans and scuffed boots, he possessed large hands, extending out from his long sleeve shirt. His hands were red from the sun, and rough, as evidenced by their bulging knuckles and thick calluses. He had sandy-colored hair that hung to his shoulders and a drooping moustache that gave his long face a mournful look. He also wore a wide brimmed hat with a high cone-like crown and a thin leather strap under his chin to hold it in place. I had never seen such a hat before and asked him about it.

"The greasers kind of come up with it," he said. "They call it a *sombrero*. Helps keep the sun off. The sun is awful unforgiving here. You don't have a hat, ma'am?"

"It was lost on the way here," I said. I did not wish to tell the story of the cows trampling it. The sun indeed was quite bright. I raised my hand to shield my eyes and spied Mr. Fairchild. He was speaking with the baggage handler who appeared to be giving him directions, and then Mr. Fairchild took one his books from his bag. I thought he was offering it as thanks but as we walked past them, I heard Mr. Fairchild trying to sell the copy to the handler. I also caught the smell of liquor about Mr. Fairchild. So potent was the aroma I concluded he must have spilled a significant amount on his clothes during his respite in the Annex Saloon.

We stepped off the platform and Mr. Jessup guided me past waiting carriages, wagons and horses.

He said, "I wanted to tell you I am very sorry about your sister. She was a good woman, a fine mother. And, well, we're glad you're here, ma'am."

"Thank you for that." I wanted to ask him about Brigid, about what had happened. Anxious as I was, I knew I should wait to hear it from Charles first. It was the proper thing to do. I would ask Charles to take me to see Brigid's grave, as well.

Reaching the surrey, I saw it was a handsome thing with two wide tufted leather seats, front and back. Enough room for a small family. There were two polished brass lamps, one each mounted to either side of the front seat. The two-horse team stood calmly. A pair of sorrel mares they were, one marked with a white face, the other with two white forefeet. Mr. Jessup apologized that the surrey had no canopy. "It's being replaced, ma'am."

"Did something happen?"

Helping me into the rear seat he said, "It was the day your sister was buried. After the ceremony we came back home and Mrs. Medrano, she's the housekeeper, she took the children inside. Mr. Preston said he had to go to Mr. Catron's office. Important business. He and Mr. Catron work together."

Charles left his children after burying their mother, I thought disgustedly.

Mr. Jessup continued. "I brought the surrey back around to take him into town, but he told me he would drive himself. Sometimes he did that. Mr. Catron's office is on the *plaza* and that day, workmen were trimming the trees there. I'll show you. We'll go by it on the way to the house."

"I'm sorry, Mr. Jessup, but what is a *plaza*?"

"Mex talk. Means public square. Anyway, Mr. Preston left the surrey where men were preparing to saw branches off a tree. They told him he shouldn't leave it there, but he paid them no mind. They started sawing, trying to be careful, and this branch they were cutting, a big heavy one, it just snapped. Broke right off."

"Oh, no," I said.

"Yes, ma'am. It crushed the top, bent some props, broke others, and scared the horses. Fortunately, a couple of the workers were able to catch them before they bolted."

"It was fortunate no one was sitting in it then."

"Very fortunate," he said and placed my carpetbag next to me on the seat. "When Mr. Preston came back home, he was angrier than I've ever seen him. Said he was going to sue everybody. The workmen, the city." Mr. Jessup shook his head. "He told me to order a new canopy for the surrey. We're still waiting on it. Strange about that branch, though."

"But branches do break," I said.

"That is true, ma'am. But in all the trimming they did that day, that branch was the only one that got away from the workmen."

He reached under the front seat, pulled out a black umbrella and held it out to me.

"I don't understand," I said. "There isn't a cloud in the sky."

He pointed up at the sky. "The sun, ma'am. Like I said, it's awful unforgiving around here, especially on fair skin like yours. If you don't mind my saying."

I opened the umbrella. The shade was a welcome comfort, I had to admit, but it did feel odd holding an open umbrella in the full brightness of day.

"And the air is a mite thinner here, too," he said as he climbed up into the driver's seat. "You are sitting about seven thousand feet closer to the sky than you were there back in Pittsburgh."

I took in a deep breath, but I felt no tingle of bubbles in my lungs as the train conductor had suggested I might. However, I did feel a little tightness in my chest. Perhaps after that passed, the bubbles would come.

"Tell me, Mr. Jessup," I said, "how long have you worked for my sister?"

"About eight years now. Come to think of it, Mrs. Preston had just had her second child when Mr. Preston hired me." He gently snapped the leather reins and guided the horses away from the depot. "I patched up his roof after a bad hailstorm and he offered me a job as caretaker. Said he could use a dependable worker. I've got plenty more caretaking responsibilities now at the new house."

"Where did he and my sister live before?"

"Place over on Johnson Street, close by where the Methodists built their church." He grunted and shook his head. "I heard Mr. Preston got a good deal on that old house. Bought it from Mr. Catron who got it as part of a court settlement proceeding. Least that's what I heard. Anyway, that house needed considerable work when they moved in. But there's always work to be done, keeping things in good repair around here. Patching, replacing rotted wood and the like. This sun here—"

"Is unforgiving," I cut in, suddenly feeling embarrassed, not having meant to complete his comment like that.

He chuckled and said, "You're catching on, ma'am."

# Chapter Eight

We were on a narrow, rutted road that had barely room for two carriages to pass each other. I noted but a handful of tall buildings, perhaps three stories high, standing off in the distance in several different directions. Mr. Jessup said they were hotels, mostly. There was also what appeared to be an imposing square tower of some kind, but I lost sight of it and the other buildings as the road suddenly dipped. We passed some small huts and also weedy fields where goats grazed, a few raising their heads as we went by.

A wooden bridge lay ahead. A gentle river ran beneath it. Few trees stood along its banks here.

"That's the Santa Fe River," Mr. Jessup said. "You'll see it again. Mr. Preston's property backs up to it."

We were almost across the bridge when I heard a loud clattering. A horse and carriage appeared from around a long hut and came racing toward us, dust rising in its wake. Mr. Jessup uttered an oath and snapped the reins. The man driving that carriage put his whip to his horse. He was not slowing down! We barely made it to the other side, the carriage nearly colliding with us.

"Slow down, you greaser!" Mr. Jessup shouted, trying to control the horses.

I caught sight of a frail old woman seated in the back of the buggy.

She was dressed all in black, her face deeply creased, her mouth open and toothless.

"Are you all right, ma'am?" Mr. Jessup asked.

"Yes," I said, catching my breath. "It, it startled me is all."

"Some of these greasers act like they still run things around here. Expect everybody ought to get out of their way and bow when they pass by." He cocked his head at me. "You sure you're all right, ma'am? You look a mite pale."

"No. It's all right," I said, though still a little shaken. "But I'm afraid I'm confused."

"About what, ma'am?"

"What are greasers?"

"Mexicans, ma'am."

I was uncertain what to make of his explanation. I knew nothing of Mexicans.

He reached down and brought up a canteen. "I have water here, ma'am, and a clean cup to drink from if you'd like."

"Thank you, I'm fine. But I think that poor woman was probably frightened to death."

"Woman, ma'am?"

"Yes, the one that was riding in that carriage."

Mr. Jessup frowned and shook his head. "I didn't see any woman."

How could he not? I had seen her as plainly as I could see him.

Making a turn onto another path, no wider than a Pittsburgh alleyway, Mr. Jessup announced we were on San Francisco Street. A most surprising and splendid sight greeted me. Far ahead rising up at the end of the street dwarfing everything within sight was unmistakably a house of God. At the apex of the pitched roof stood a stone cross. Two bell towers braced the façade of the church. One had only a partially built belfry, and a tall crane was lowering a large square, reddish-colored stone it held suspended over it into place. The other tower was the one I had spotted briefly before, on leaving the depot. It, too, stood unfinished, its flat top giving it a hard, stunted appearance. Even so, with the tree covered mountains rising behind it and the blue sky above, it made for a beautiful sight.

Mr. Jessup told me it was the Catholic cathedral. "You saw where they've been quarrying much of the stone for it when you changed trains to come up here. That mountain they've been cutting into?"

"Oh, yes, I did." So that explained the mountain with the cleaved sections.

"The bishop, or no, the archbishop I guess he is now, he picked the right town to build his new church."

"I don't understand. The right town?"

"Santa Fe. Means holy faith. That archbishop's got to have a boat full of that kind of faith to build something like that out here in this country. That's for certain."

"Well, a grand sight it is," I said. "And the spires on the towers will make a fine finishing touch."

Mr. Jessup chuckled. "Pardon me, ma'am, but there won't be any spires."

"What do you mean?"

"I mean the archbishop; he's not going to build them."

"And why not? They would be magnificent." I could almost see them reaching up far into the sky, like twin beacons pointing the way to heaven.

"Two reasons, the way I heard it. First, we get some fierce thunderstorms here, and those spires he was planning, they were going to be built out of wood. Lightning comes with those thunderstorms and, if lightning struck, the mess if those spires caught fire would be considerable."

That was understandable, though unfortunate. "And the second reason?"

"He's plain out of money. It's taken him better than fifteen years to get this far. He'll be lucky to get that other tower finished at all, you ask me."

Mr. Jessup's story saddened me. And yet, it seemed so odd that a house of God would be left flawed that way.

San Francisco Street was a main thoroughfare of town and a sad-looking avenue it was. Rough wooden sidewalks, uneven in many places, lined both sides of the street. So did buildings, and there was not a pitched roof among them. All flat. A scattered few rose two stories high, like Herlow's Hotel with its decrepit-looking balcony, but most were only one story with narrow doors and windows. A thick ugly kind of brown plaster covered the walls. Ragged cracks showed on many of them. My convent in Pittsburgh was like a palace compared to these places. I asked Mr. Jessup what the buildings were made of.

"Mud and straw," he said. "They mix them together into bricks and let the sun dry them. *Adobe*, they call it."

I had never heard of such a thing.

He pointed at one place as we went by. "See the bricks showing there?"

Big pieces of the brown plaster had broken off from around the window leaving long mud-colored bricks exposed. More bricks were in evidence at the corners of the place where that plaster had fallen away.

"They may not be much to look at," he went on, "but I'll tell you, that *adobe* keeps things good and warm inside during the cold winters, and surprisingly cool in the summers. Funny thing how that is, too, because you wouldn't think these greasers could figure out—"

The sound of metal clanging drew my attention down a side street. In the doorway of a livery stable, a blacksmith with hammered out a quick tattoo on an anvil, while a farrier with a big belly put nails between his lips, preparing to shoe a horse tied nearby. The farrier raised his head and looked at me. He had a hole in his head where he was missing an eye.

"—and all of this," I heard Mr. Jessup say, "the whole Territory, it used to belong to Mexico. But not anymore. Some say after we took it away from the Mexicans we made it better. Others say we ought to give it back to them, but I don't know."

Passing an alleyway, I saw seven or eight mules. At least they looked like mules to me with their large heads and alert ears, big eyes, stubby legs and short tails. But Mr. Jessup called them *burros* and said they were smaller than mules, "and smarter by far." I had seen their mule cousins on the streets of Pittsburgh hitched to wagons. The difference was that these *burros* were laden with bundles of crooked sticks tied to their backs across a packsaddle. The bundles of sticks were for sale. Their owners laughed and yelled and waved their arms at each other. Such vulgar antics. But I could not understand why the men were wearing blankets. And the speech of these men! It sounded like the alphabet gone mad.

"Do you know what they're saying, Mr. Jessup?" I asked.

"Greaser talk," he said. "Most likely they're swapping lies." He raised his hand and said something in a torrent of odd sounds. The men responded to him in kind and addressed him by an odd term. Whatever they said made Mr. Jessup laugh.

"Mr. Jessup, what was that name he called you?"

"*Gringo.*"

I asked him what it meant.

"Hard to say, ma'am. A lot of greasers call us Americans *gringos.*

Some folks think it means something bad. I pay it no mind. Just greaser talk to me."

"Why do you call these people greasers?" I asked. I wanted to understand his nearly constant use of the word.

He shrugged and said, "That's what they are, many of them."

"And what is that exactly?"

"Well, ma'am, they got the name on account of a dirty job they're willing to do."

"What job?"

"They get a bucket, fill it with grease, crawl under a wagon and grease the axles. As nasty a job as there is. Greaser. Mex. All the same to me. And from what I can tell, more than a few of them look like they apply that grease to their hair."

I made no response as I considered what he had said. Mr. Jessup turned. I must have had a most pensive expression on my face for he asked me if anything was wrong. I told him, not unkindly, that it did not seem right calling these people a name like that. "God created all of us in His image," I said.

"Well, I wouldn't know much about that, ma'am. Me and God, we parted ways after Gettysburg. But as to name calling, it's just my way of keeping different folks straight in my head."

"I prefer to think that a decent man is a decent man, regardless of his origins," I said.

"That's a fine sentiment. You know, when I come out this way after the war, I didn't care much for greasers. But I can tell you they aren't half bad. From what I've seen, many a white man here is on the make ready to pluck taxpayer and rascal alike, though some are honest enough. A Mex, on the other hand, well, some are liars and thieves, but there are those that will divvy his plate of beans with any stranger, and not expect a thing in return for his trouble."

My Father would have called Mr. Jessup a colorful character. Mother would have been less complimentary. To me, Mr. Jessup was the most incorrigible a man I had ever met. I had to admit though, he did possess a unique way of making his point. I thought perhaps I might try to persuade him later to adjust his vocabulary, but for the time being I decided it best to leave it at that.

## Chapter Nine

We passed a cobbler's shop, a dry goods store, a gambling hall, and a place called the Old Reliable Jewelry House where a sign proclaimed E. Andrews proprietor and dentist. Further up the street I saw signs hanging from eaves for at least five saloons. There was even a sign with a painted arrow pointing the way to a bowling alley.

A short man with long chin whiskers and an odd-looking little black cap on his head was washing the windows of his shop. Painted letters on the window read Chinese Laundry. The funny looking lines painted below it I took for the same words in Chinese.

"Mr. Jing! You still in business today?" Jessup called out.

The short man turned, glared at Mr. Jessup, and went to back to his washing with an urgency.

"He doesn't seem to like you," I said.

"No, he doesn't." Jessup said. "That little Chinaman ought to stick to raising rice, not claiming he can—"

A hard jolt startled me. The horses shied and Mr. Jessup pulled back on the reins to avoid a collision with another wagon emerging from a side alley ahead of us. The two rough-looking men sitting on the driver's bench in that wagon paid us no mind.

Mr. Jessup voiced an indelicate suggestion about their parentage then begged my pardon for his language and we began to move again.

That wagon the men drove ahead of us was stacked with crates marked FIREWORKS in black letters. Doubting they were for next year's Fourth of July celebration, I asked Mr. Jessup about them.

"Yes, ma'am. This Saturday is the feast of St. Francis of Assisi. The archbishop, John Lamy is his name, he—"

"Pardon me," I interrupted. "Did you say his name was Lamy?"

"Yes, ma'am."

"Would he be named for the depot where I changed trains?"

"He is, ma'am. It used to be called Galisteo Junction, but they changed it in his honor. If I was him, I'd be insulted."

"Well, it's far from grand," I said, "but why name that place after him?"

"You remember me mentioning the mountain that's been cut into?"

"I do."

"It's one of the places they get the stone to build his cathedral. They've been hauling it by wagon from there for a long time." He reached down and brought up his canteen again. "Sure you wouldn't like some water, ma'am?"

I thanked him and said I was fine.

"As I was saying, John Lamy come here from France. He named the cathedral after that Francis fellow and every year he marks the day. The whole town comes out. They shoot off the fireworks over at old Fort Marcy. That's the Yankee fort north of town, except they packed up and left it some time ago. Those two in the wagon up there, they were blue bellies at the fort and think rather highly of themselves." He shook his head disgustedly. "But I was speaking of the feast. The St. Francis band plays out in front of the cathedral. They play pretty good. And along the street here they set bonfires to light the way to the festivities. *Gran celebración*."

"Pardon me?

"Means big celebration in Mex. You stay around long enough you can't help picking up some of their lingo."

The fireworks wagon turned on a street marked Lincoln and Mr. Jessup said, "Good riddance, you damn blue bellies." He looked back over his shoulder at me. "Pardon my language, ma'am. And here, this is the *plaza*."

A wide, open area appeared to my left. More long mud dwellings fronted it on every side, though here and there some supported a second story. But that open space had the look of a respectable park maybe three hundred feet wide. A white picket fence surrounded it, and there were walkways and dozens of trees. But, as Mr. Jessup had said, every one of those trees had been trimmed back, their thick trunks looking like burly sentinels standing guard over the center of town. Several gas lampposts stood around the square. They were the first I had seen here. I mentioned it to Mr. Jessup, and he informed me that coal gas had come to Santa Fe four years earlier.

"Slow but sure this town's becoming more civilized," he said. "Every year the town council loosens their purse strings, and two or three more lamps go up. Least way that's how it looks to me."

In the center of the *plaza*, an obelisk atop a stone block foundation stood nearly as tall as the truncated trees. Mr. Jessup said it was the monument to the Yankee heroes of the war. "Yankees do like their statues," he said.

A couple of fellows were giving a covered bandstand on the other side of the obelisk a fresh coat of white paint. Besides those men, there were not many people around this *plaza* at the moment. A barber dressed in a red striped vest swept out the doorway of his shop. Several women in fine clothes were taking a stroll together across the square. A clerk wearing a leather apron helped a fellow in rolled up shirtsleeves load barrels into a wagon outside an establishment called Spiegelberg Bros. General Merchandise. Next door was a bank where two dapper men in tall silk hats stood laughing over who-knew-what. One smoked a pipe. In some respects, it was not unlike Pittsburgh.

Some rough-looking cowboys on horseback rode past us. Rank was the only word to describe the smell as they passed. I heard one of them say the Exchange Hotel had good whiskey and grub. Up ahead on the right sat that hotel. I thought it looked about as inviting as a dark cave.

Glancing over to my left, I spied four women clad in simple-looking white garb, though one wore a black skirt and a couple had colorful calico shawls around their shoulders. Each had dark hair that was arranged in long locks. One had a child cradled in one arm, while another held a little boy by the hand. But each of the four women carried a clay pot balanced on top of their heads. I had never seen such a thing and I asked Mr. Jessup who the women were and what they were doing with those pots.

"They're Indians, ma'am," he said.

"Indians!" I said in astonishment.

"Nothing to worry yourself about. They aren't hostile. Farmers and pot makers, mostly. Some of the women work for folks here in town as servants. There's a fountain over near the bandstand. It's where they come to fetch water to fill those pots."

All I knew of Indians came from stories in the newspapers back in Pittsburgh. They ran reports of some savage bands still roaming the country or settled on reservations, but not as residents of towns. And the idea of balancing a big pot of water on one's head still confounded me. Looking back at them again, I saw a couple of them smoking cigars! Had Brigid on her arrival here been as baffled by this place as I was now?

"There's plenty of folks come to the *plaza* to fetch their water," Mr. Jessup said. "Others dip it out of the river or get it from one of the *acequias*."

"Pardon me. A what?"

"Like a canal. The *Diegos* built them. *Diegos* is the Spanish, ma'am. These little canals bring water to different parts of town." He chuckled. "Being as high up as we are it can be hard to imagine."

"What's hard to imagine?"

"That we're sitting square on the desert. Oh, we got the river and it's our source of water. But the desert is the desert. And it can be unforgiving, too."

I detected another distasteful odor as Mr. Jessup hurried past two Mexican men, each pushing wooden carts piled with waste and debris. Scrawny looking dogs trailed after them.

"Sorry about the smell, ma'am. Rubbish collection," he said. "As sure a sign of civilization as there could possibly be."

The two men wore fringed blankets, just like those men I had seen earlier with the burros. I managed to find my voice again and asked Mr. Jessup why these men had cut a hole in a perfectly good blanket to stick their heads through.

He burst out with a laugh, then apologized saying he meant no disrespect, only that he had thought the same thing when he saw them for the first time. "They are blankets, but they call them *serapes*," he said. "They wear them like we wear a coat. Greasers like them, and some cowboys."

What had I come to? For something to be right in this place, something else must be wrong. Clearly, things here were upside down.

"And see over there," Mr. Jessup said. "Where it says post office?"

At first I thought he was pointing at the deplorable-looking place with a long uneven covered porch, but I realized he was indicating the two-story building across from it on the corner. I saw the post office sign over the last doorway and told him so.

"Mr. Catron's office is up the stairs through the doorway next to it," he said. "And that big tree, the one there directly opposite it? That's the one the branch fell from and crushed the top of Mr. Preston's surrey."

Reaching the cathedral at the end of San Francisco Street, Mr. Jessup reined the horses to the left and then right onto another dirt road called Palace Avenue, named, I would later find out, for the Palace of the Governors, that shoddy place on the square with the uneven porch.

But I could not look away from the grandness of the cathedral. Five tall stained-glass windows were set in its long brown wall. At the base of the wall was a small cemetery marked with headstones and crosses. Behind the cathedral amid the trees was St. Vincent's Hospital and Sanitarium, tall stout-looking buildings that would not have been out of place in Pittsburgh. Several other buildings stood close by. One was an orphan asylum according to Mr. Jessup. Of course, that made me think of my girls, but I had two new charges of my own to meet shortly. In front of the hospital, two sisters dressed in black habits with black caps on their heads that looked very much like bonnets to me helped a pregnant woman down from a wagon. Not recognizing the clothing of this Order, I was about to ask Mr. Jessup about them when he inquired about the Order I belonged to. I told him that I was a postulant with the Sisters of Mercy.

"That's right. I remember now," he said. "The reason I ask is because the Sisters of Charity run this hospital and I couldn't remember which bunch of sisters Mr. Preston said you were with."

Further up ahead, I caught a glimpse of what appeared to be a stately looking place beyond a grove of trees. Mr. Jessup said it was the home of Mr. Staab who owned one of the two big merchandise stores in town. "Mr. Spiegelberg and his brothers operate the other one. We passed by their store on the *plaza*. They're all Dutchies."

Those names sounded more German than Dutch to me. Over the last ten years, many Germans had come to Pittsburgh, and I had heard men there call anyone who came from Holland or Germany and maybe a couple of other countries Dutchies.

"And do you know where they hail from, Mr. Jessup?" I asked.

"Yes, ma'am. A place called Prussia, I think. They sell good, reliable wares at both their stores. They're Jews, you know."

"Oh?"

"They've donated a lot of money to the archbishop for his cathedral. The Spiegelberg boys opened a bank, too. Right next to their store. Willi, he's the youngest one, he runs the store, and his brother Lehman is president of the bank. Matter of fact, we passed Willi's house back there."

Turning to look, I saw mostly trees and another house already blocking my view of the place.

"And this old tree here on the left," he went on, "they almost hanged a man from it."

"Hanged, did you say?" Not only was this place upside down but uncivilized, as well.

"Almost hanged. They hauled him up, but the rope snapped."

"Good Lord."

"The law came running and heated words were exchanged with the leader of the vigilance committee.

"Vigilance committee. You mean a lynch mob, don't you?"

"Oh, no. Ollie Tibbs was guilty. He robbed and murdered Will Embree after losing about sixty dollars to him in a card game. Will Embree was well liked around here, so well liked that to assure Tibbs a fair hearing, the judge ordered him taken to Albuquerque for trial. A shame."

"And why do you say that?"

"Tibbs escaped from the jail down there and hasn't been heard of since." He grunted. "Strange about that rope breaking, though."

"Strange?"

"It was brand new, but it snapped like old, frayed hemp. Some say peculiar things happen around here all the time claiming it's on account of they built the town on Indian burial grounds." He shrugged. "There's those that believe in that kind of foolishness."

What had I come to?

We turned onto a rutted road, passed a windmill, and went a short way through a wooded area. As we cleared the trees, the road before us led directly to my destination. Brigid mentioned in a few of her letters that Charles was doing well as an attorney, but nothing she had written could have prepared me for this.

The house was three stories high and made of red brick. White stone blocks climbed up the corners of the place as though holding it together. It was topped with a mansard roof, gray in color, with cast iron cresting along the edges. Three single gabled windows extended out from the slope of the roof on the front of the house as well as the sides from what I could see. The windows on the other two floors were arranged in pairs with window hoods shaped like eyebrows and supported by carved brackets. A tower, rectangular in shape and four stories tall, stood at the front right corner of the house. It, too, was topped with a sloped roof and had pairs of windows with eyebrow-shaped hoods at each floor. An elaborate wooden porch yawned out over the front entrance and extended over to the left side of the front of the house. Beautiful large trees grew around at the sides of the house. Mr. Jessup said they were cottonwoods and cedars. The cedars remained green while the leaves of the cottonwoods were already ablaze in bright yellow.

Grand and breathtaking my sister's house was. But on drawing closer a more disquieting feeling descended, like a voice whispering to me to go away at once.

Something was waiting.

# Chapter Ten

**M**r. Jessup pulled the horses to a stop on the gravel driveway in front of the house and helped me down from the surrey. Closing the umbrella, I gave it back to him with thanks.

"After you, ma'am," Mr. Jessup said.

My carpetbag in hand, I proceeded along the pathway, the gravel crunching softly under my feet. Mr. Jessup offered his arm as I climbed the stairs. Reaching the porch landing, the ornate paired doors opened and a slight woman wearing a plain dark dress stepped out. I guessed her to be about fifty years of age. Her skin was coppery in color, and her thick raven black hair, streaked with traces of gray, was pulled back and fastened into a bun resting on the nape of her neck. She had high cheekbones and an aquiline nose. Beauty had not abandoned her.

She spoke five or six words in Spanish, but all I could understand was when I heard her say my last name, Danaher. I stood there flummoxed, not knowing what to say.

"Pardon me," she said, her embarrassment showing, "I forget sometimes not everyone speaks Spanish. I bid you welcome. I am Mrs. Consuela Medrano, the housekeeper. Please, come inside." Her voice rose and fell with a resonant cadence.

Behind me I heard Mr. Jessup say, "I'll go see to the children."

"Oh, are they here?" I asked. I was ready to meet them.

"No," Mrs. Medrano said. "They are at school. He will go get them."

I turned to thank Mr. Jessup for bringing me to the house. He was already up in the driver's seat of the surrey.

"My pleasure, ma'am," he said, touching the brim of his big hat and drove off back down the driveway.

Mrs. Medrano extended her hand and asked if she could take my bag. Not used to such things I hesitated, then handed it to her and she led me inside.

The entryway opened to a wide foyer. My Lord, I thought on seeing it. A beautiful Persian rug in colors of black, orange and white spread over the dark wood floor. Two small tables stood against opposite walls, and behind both tables hung matching mirrors with gilt frames. A glass chandelier hung from the ceiling braced with elaborate crown molding. Dark wood paneling to waist height covered the walls running the length of the foyer and along the hallway straight ahead leading to the promise of more rooms. Light green colored wallpaper decorated the remainder of the foyer and hallway.

Further into the foyer, a staircase wound up along the wall. The banister was so ornately carved I was almost reluctant to touch it. To the right at the foot of the staircase was an entryway that opened into a sitting room. Several landscape paintings hung on the walls. Green velvet covered the chairs and couch. Across the foyer on the left stood the entryway to another room where floor-to-ceiling bookshelves covered the wall, enough for a small library.

I was about to ask Mrs. Medrano if Charles was at home when I heard his voice call out from that room. "In here. Come."

The hairs on the back of my neck bristled and my face flushed red. I had not forgotten why I was here, or the questions that I had waited to ask for almost two thousand miles. But I was not a dog to be whistled for, let alone commanded. Clasping one hand over the other in front of me, I stood and waited. Quietly. Unmoving.

A worried look came over Mrs. Medrano's face, uncertain of what to do.

I heard a frustrated sigh, followed by footsteps crossing the wooden floor of the library.

Charles appeared at the entryway. In his hand he held a piece of paper, what I guessed to be a letter from the way it was creased. His clothes, like his house, bespoke wealth. I noticed the gold stickpin in his tie. He was still a handsome man, and I suspected he was still keenly aware of it. His hair was lacquered into place, and he now wore a moustache, the ends of which were waxed and tapered to fine points. His dark eyes looked me up and down. I could sense his disdain. At the convent we were instructed that Christ had commanded that we love one another as He loved us. Looking at my brother-in-law, I could not help myself. I detested Charles immediately.

"Well, Catherine. So, you've finally arrived," he said.

You left me little choice, I thought, but held my tongue.

"Come in, then," he said. "Mrs. Medrano, bring her something to drink, will you? She must be thirsty." He turned abruptly and went back into the library.

Mrs. Medrano said she would return after she put my bag in my room and started up the stairs.

I stepped into the library. It was a man's room, as my Father would have said, for it smelled of whisky and cigars. Shelves filled with books did indeed cover much of the walls. There was a great open fireplace. Two windows faced the front of the house and two others looked out on the trees at the side of the house. One of those was open about a foot. Heavy drapes of dark blue were tied back on either side of the windows while sheer blue curtains that hung separately behind the drapes extended down to the floor, allowing filtered shafts of sunlight through. Several solid-looking chairs and a couch were covered in blue velvet matching the drapes. But my interest at this moment was not in books or drapes or chairs.

Charles was already seated in a heavy chair, his legs crossed, reading the letter he still held, and enjoying it from the look on his face. It was as though I wasn't even standing there! The ill-mannered snob. Well, he was the one wanted me here, and now I was, and I would have some answers.

"Charles, how did my sister die?" I did my best to keep the edge out of my voice.

He folded the letter, slipped it inside his jacket pocket and said, "An accident."

There was not so much as a hint of sadness in his voice or an expression of remorse.

When he offered no further explanation, I asked him to please explain this "accident."

He told me of the circumstances in the same cold manner. It had happened the first day she came to the new house. He said that in the months he had spent having this house built, he did not wish her to see it until it was completed and furnished. The day it was finally ready he brought her and the children to it, but he could not stay, having to leave that afternoon for Denver on important business.

"It is my understanding," he said, "that in the evening Brigid went out for a walk down by the river where my property ends. She was found unconscious later, on the riverbank."

"Was she in the habit of taking walks in the evening by herself?" I asked.

"Yes, she was. She particularly enjoyed that part of the day, the quiet and the solitude."

"But didn't anyone think it was strange when she didn't return to the house after it was dark?"

He made a show of folding his hands together then said, "After her walks, Brigid was also in the habit of sitting and watching the stars come out. Now, as I was saying, a boy and his father found her on the riverbank. The boy's dog had gotten loose, and they went looking for it. Hearing the dog barking, they followed the sound and found him by Brigid's body. They brought her to the house and the doctor was summoned. Doctor Symington said she had taken water into her lungs and—"

"You mean she drowned?"

"Allow me to finish. She was still breathing but unconscious. She had also struck her head on a rock, or perhaps had been struck by one. He found other scrapes and bruises, as well. She lay in a coma at St. Vincent's Hospital for nearly a month before she died."

"The night she was attacked, were the authorities called?"

"Of course," he said. "The chief of police came, and the sheriff. They are working together to apprehend the culprit."

"And what of the children?"

"What about them?"

"Where were they when their mother was down by the river?"

"Mrs. Medrano said they were in the house with her. Isn't that true?" he said, looking past me.

I turned and saw Mrs. Medrano waiting at the entryway. She held a glass of water in her hand.

"Yes, it is true," she said and set the glass down on a nearby table for me. "A sad day." She quickly left the room.

"I assure you," Charles said, getting up from his chair, "all that could be done to care for your sister was done. When she died, it was merciful." The way he said it he sounded as though he had been somehow inconvenienced because of her.

Infuriated I was by his manner. As he had not seen fit to mention it and as I was of a mind to know with certainty, I asked, with as much civility as I could muster, "Did my sister receive the sacrament of the anointing of the sick and die in a state of grace, then?"

He waited a moment before saying that yes, she had.

I did not want to look at his face. Wanting some air, I went to the open window.

The sound of horses caught my attention and I saw Mr. Jessup go by in the surrey. A modest stable stood toward the rear of the house. And beyond it I saw something surprising. Rose bushes. Beds of them in long rows, still in bloom, a considerable garden of them.

"I had those planted for your sister while the house was being built," Charles said, and I realized he was standing next to me by the window.

"Yes." I tried my best to sound polite. "She loved roses."

"Indeed." His inflection was clipped, as though my comment was somehow needless.

Charles was a churlish toad. What had Brigid seen in him? I had no wish now to ask him to take me to the cemetery to see Brigid's grave. Any remark he made at her graveside might well result in my doing something regrettable. And such a thing would be an insult to my sister. Surely, Mr. Jessup would have the time to take me to her final resting place at some point, and gladly, too.

I heard the front door open and the sound of footsteps out in the foyer.

"Mr. Preston." It was Mrs. Medrano's voice. "The children are home."

Of course, Mr. Jessup had gone to get them from school. I turned and saw Mrs. Medrano usher the children into the library.

"Yes. My children," Charles said. "Matthew and Anne."

Anne. I could not help but smile. That was Mother's name. Dressed in a blue print dress and a white pinafore, Anne was eight with chestnut red hair, like Brigid, and a face just as pretty. Her cheekbones appeared as though carved by shadows.

"This is your Aunt Catherine," Charles said. "Tell her you're glad to meet her."

Anne smiled and did as he said.

Matthew, two years older than his sister, barely glanced up as he mumbled his greeting. I could not tell if he was shy, or if it due to a glumness on his part. He wore a white shirt with dark coat and trousers. I thought it might be the uniform of the school he attended. Like his father, Matthew was a handsome boy. I could only hope the similarity to his father ended there and that he possessed his mother's sweet disposition.

"All right then," Charles said. "Children, your aunt will see to you until my return."

I snapped my head at him. "You're leaving?"

He stared at me and pursed his lips. He glanced at Mrs. Medrano. She whispered to Matthew and Anne and guided them out of the room.

"I am leaving tomorrow morning," he said. "I have new business back in Denver that requires my immediate attention."

"And how long will you be away?"

"At least three weeks, perhaps four."

"Four weeks? I don't understand. Your telegram said—"

"Depositions take time," he said curtly. "Contracts require careful review. Legal matters cannot be rushed. Now, I must go to my office in town to make preparations for my journey tomorrow. On my return we shall deal with other matters."

He took a valise that sat on the floor next to his chair and left the house calling out to Mr. Jessup to bring the surrey around.

The heat rose in my face. I had more questions for Charles, and plenty more I wanted to say to him, but it would have to wait until he returned that evening.

"Please," I heard Mrs. Medrano say. I turned. She wore a sheepish expression. I could not blame her. I was a stranger here. This situation with Charles was a family matter and this quarrel must have sounded rude and unseemly to her.

"Yes?" I said, trying to calm myself down.

"Come with me. I will take you to your room."

That would be a relief. I had had quite enough of the smell of cigars and whisky. And arrogance.

## Chapter Eleven

"It was your sister's. I thought you would like it while you are here with us," Mrs. Medrano said, indicating the rocking chair sitting in the corner of the bedroom where I would stay. A quilt was draped over the back of the chair. "She sat in this chair and nursed the children. Many times I would find she had slept the night in it, wrapped in the quilt."

I ran my fingers tenderly over the soft quilt. A sadness welled up in me and I stepped away to look about the room.

Mrs. Medrano opened a cedar chest at the foot of the bed and pulled out a blanket. "The nights have started to get colder. And there is plenty more wood for your fireplace." She pointed at the split wood stacked in the iron basket by the hearth. A comfortable fire already burned in the ornate fireplace. Mrs. Medrano said Mr. Jessup had seen to it.

"He places the wood and kindling inside each fireplace, so they are ready for the night. In the morning he cleans them out," she said, adding that matches to light the kindling were in the small brass canister on top of the mantel. "Mr. Preston wanted coal burning fireplaces but your sister say she and the children would not live in the house if he did."

"What was her objection to coal?"

"She did not like the smell. Very bitter." She waved her hand.

"How did Mr. Preston take to that?"

She wore a serious expression. "He did not like it. Mr. Staab's house has coal fireplaces, he say, and Mr. Spiegelberg's house and a few others. He told her it will be much easier to keep the house warm. The pipes, they carry the hot gas from the coal furnace to the fireplaces in each room. But Mrs. Preston say no, she like the smell of the burning wood." She shrugged. "I think she worried the house might explode, or something."

My room was situated at the back of the house on a corner on the second floor. It was used as a guest room, Mrs. Medrano told me. Anne's room was next to mine, and Matthew's was next to hers. The second-floor tower room was a playroom for them, which was where they were at the moment. Across the hallway were two other rooms. One was Charles's bedroom. The other had been Brigid's. I asked Mrs. Medrano where her room was, and she said she it was on the third floor. "It is right above yours and looks very much the same."

There were two sets of windows in my room. I could see the cathedral from the windows facing to the west. Looking out the other set revealed more of the rose garden, as well as another building made of red brick. It was much smaller than the main house being only one story and had a wide chimney at one end. Mrs. Medrano said it was the kitchen and cook's quarters.

"I am doing the cooking for a few weeks along with my household chores," she said.

"Did something happen to the cook?"

"Oh, no. Mrs. Ortiz is fine. But she is caring for her father who is very old and lives alone. He took a bad fall and broke his hip."

"I can help you with the meals, if you'd like," I said.

"No, that is not necessary. I can manage," she said with an easy confidence. "The children. They need you. But you get settled now. You must be tired. I will go get supper ready. I hope beef is to your liking."

"That sounds fine."

"*Bueno.*"

"I'm sorry?"

"Forgive me again. It is Spanish for good."

She smiled and pulled the door closed behind her, leaving me alone in the room.

I said the word out loud. *Bueno*. It was easy enough. Perhaps Mr. Jessup was right, that I would learn some of the language while I was here.

The few things I had to unpack barely took up a corner in the top drawer of the dresser. And the armoire that could easily hold a dozen dresses remained tenantless, except for my carpetbag.

Using the pitcher of water that rested on the dressing table, I filled the basin and rinsed off my face.

The walls and drapes of my room were what some might call apricot in color, but after I had dried my face, those apricot-colored walls glowed with light and the furniture gleamed a dusky red. Going to the window I could not help but take a sudden breath in wonder. I had never seen such a remarkable sunset. The light in this place was long and luminous, colors bolder and sharper. And yet those colors are also delicate as gossamer. Surely, it was a gift from God.

\* \* \*

Downstairs, the dining room held a long table with tall chairs. The mood of the children was as heavy as the table, and I decided not to press the matter. Lighted candles in the chandelier overhead cast a soft pleasing glow.

Mrs. Medrano had prepared a supper of stew that consisted of roasted beef and potatoes and greens. She said Mr. Preston told her to make it bland and asked me if it was to my liking. I told her it was delicious, though I did not mention she was correct about the blandness. I asked her why Charles had instructed her as to the preparation and she said some people were not used to Mexican cooking. She mentioned chili peppers and some other ingredients I had never heard of, but I told her it would not be necessary to alter her recipes on my account.

She hesitated. "Are you sure?"

"I am."

After supper, the children prepared their school lessons for the following day. My displeasure with Charles had not diminished, but I put that aside to perform my duties to help and care for the children. Anne brought me her spelling lesson and asked me to go down the list of twenty words to see that she pronounced and spelled each one correctly. The word "quiver" proved difficult as she spelled it with the letter C instead of Q. But I was pleased to find her a bright child, having no trouble with any other words such as lantern, umbrella or rattle.

When I asked Matthew if he needed any help with his arithmetic, he said curtly that he did not.

Later, Mrs. Medrano helped me put the children to bed. After saying his prayers, Matthew remained petulant, giving his back to us once in his bed. In Anne's room, we listened as she finished her prayers. She added my name to those she asked God to bless, and I was truly touched, if not a little surprised. Clutching her golden-haired dolly, Anne climbed into bed. As I helped her with her covers, I told her how glad I was to be here with her and her brother. "Your

Mother is up in heaven watching over us, and I'm here to help her do that."

She smiled, though I saw sadness in her eyes. It was to be expected. We all needed time.

I tried to stay awake until Charles returned but I was so tired. It had been a long day. Waiting downstairs in the tower sitting room, I was dozing in one of the green velvet covered chairs, the fire Mr. Jessup had lighted in the fireplace warming me. Shadows and light flickered and danced about the room. The grandfather clock chimed, rousing me. It was already half past ten and Charles had not yet come home. I needed sleep. My questions for Charles would have to wait until morning.

Up in my room, the atmosphere felt comfortable, and I saw no need to add more wood to the fireplace. Tired though I was, I opened the Divine Office and read the nightly prayers. Afterwards, I got on my knees and prayed at my bedside, asking God for the strength to follow His will, for His guidance in caring for Matthew and Anne, and for as much patience as He could give me in dealing with Charles. Oh, and also to help Mr. Jessup become a more tolerant man.

Bringing my Mother's silver crucifix to my mouth, I kissed it then climbed into bed. Not only was this bed much larger than what I slept on at the convent, but also much more comfortable, sinfully so, for I sank deep into the feather mattress. I warned myself not to get too used to it.

Closing my eyes, I was keenly aware of the quiet in the house, and the stillness outside. The machine sounds of Pittsburgh never ceased, and the rattles and clinks of the trains on my journey had been constant. But here, now, the silence was peculiar, almost unnatural. Being exhausted, though, I fell asleep quickly.

I had no idea what the hour was when a strange sound coming from outside awakened me. It sounded like crying. A woman. Or was it a child? It was coming from down in the garden.

Going to the window, I pulled open the drapes. The crying stopped. Perhaps I had imagined it. The white moon was full and high in the coal black sky. All appeared still, and I realized I had not had a look at the entire garden before this moment. Could it possibly cover so much ground? Moonlight can play odd tricks upon the eye. I rubbed away any errant sleep from my eyes. Looking out the window again, I saw the long black shadows the moonlight created by the trees and bushes and what looked like a trellis, too, standing near the center of the garden. I would have a better look in the morning. Wait. Something was moving. A black shape in the garden, floating above it, as big as a man, but how could that be? It turned toward the house. The shape kept coming, gaining speed. It disappeared from sight. I leaned closer to the window, staring down, trying to follow its progress when a deep blackness suddenly filled the window. Gasping, I jerked back. The blackness was gone in that instant.

A chill overtook me, icy to the bone it was, and vanished as quickly as it had come.

My heart beat quickly as I stepped cautiously to the window, peering through it from side to side and top to bottom, anticipating seeing something clinging to the house. I saw nothing. The cook's quarters and garden appeared still, as well. Had my eyes played tricks on me? I saw movement again, as though some shape shuddered atop a tree limb near the cook's house. The shape spread itself open and disappeared into the night. Was it a bird of some kind? A large owl perhaps, or a raven? It had to be.

Drawing the drapes closed, I sat on the edge of the bed. Dying red embers glowed faintly in the fireplace. Being so tired I believed my eyes had played tricks on me at first.

I slipped between the sheets and closed my eyes. Quiet enveloped the house.

# Chapter Twelve

"Mr. Preston has already gone," Mrs. Medrano said.

"And when did he leave?" I asked, my irritation rising. I glanced at the clock on the fireplace mantle in the dining room where we stood. The clock hands read ten minutes before seven.

"I don't know," she said. "But he left this on the table by the front door." She reached into her apron pocket and pulled out an envelope. My name was written on it.

I had questions, things I needed to know concerning the children, his children! Charles knew it and he ran off before the sun came up. Did he even tell Matthew and Anne good-bye? From what I had witnessed thus far with Charles, I sorely doubted it. There was nothing to be done about any of it now.

I opened the envelope. It was not even a letter, only instructions. If I required money, I was to go see Mr. Lehman Spiegelberg at the Second National Bank of Santa Fe. The care of the children was completely at my discretion. If I had any questions, I was instructed to consult Mrs. Medrano. That was all he wrote. Nothing more. The miserable man.

"Mrs. Medrano, I need your help," I said. Assisting her with setting the table I asked her my questions and she answered them. The children were usually up by quarter past seven and saw to dressing themselves. Matthew attended St. Michael's College for boys and Anne went to the Loretto Academy for girls. I was correct that Matthew's white shirt and dark coat and trousers were the uniform that St. Michael's required the boys to wear. Loretto Academy had no uniform requirement for their girls. The children had study time and play time. They went to bed by eight o'clock.

"How are they doing in school?" I asked.

"Oh, they like school," Mrs. Medrano said. "They do well. But losing their mother that way, it has been very hard on them."

"Of course. Tell me, how much school did they miss?"

"Mrs. Preston, she was buried three days later. The children, they stayed home those days and went back to school the day after the funeral."

We heard the sound of feet moving about upstairs and knew the children were up. Mrs. Medrano excused herself to go out to the kitchen to finish preparing breakfast.

I had other questions, other concerns, but they would have to wait until I went into town.

"Morning, ma'am," Mr. Jessup said. He carried a load of firewood and set it down by the dining room fireplace.

"Good morning, Mr. Jessup. I wanted to ask you if you'd have some time later today. I'd like to see my sister's grave."

"Of course."

"And some other stops, too, if it would be convenient."

"When would you like to go? After I take the children to school, I have some chores, but I can hold off on those."

"When you're finished would be fine."

The children came in, dressed and ready for school.

"Is Father here?" Anne asked hopefully.

"I'm afraid he's already left," I told her.

Her tiny shoulders slumped as she took her chair at the table.

Matthew said nothing. He kept his head down, his chin thrust forward. Anger brooded in this boy.

God, please help me, I prayed.

Mrs. Medrano arrived with plates of food, setting one before each of us. Mr. Jessup did not join us, saying he had already eaten and had chores to tend to.

We said grace, thanking God for this meal, and I tried not to stare at an item on my plate. I recognized the fried eggs, and the cubes of meat were mutton. But I was unfamiliar with the round, thin brown object. Mrs. Medrano called it a *tortilla* and said she made them herself. I gathered that a kind of corn dough was somehow involved as an ingredient. She cooked the unleavened dough in a frying pan and suggested I might like to add a little butter to it as I would a slice of bread.

I wanted to ask if there wasn't any bread in the kitchen, but I did not wish to be rude. After all, I had insisted she prepare the meals as she normally would do.

Taking the tortilla in my fingers, it had the feel of hard leather, but I did as she instructed and took a bite. I was delighted at the flavorful taste.

However, she had added chili peppers to the eggs. It felt like an inferno had erupted in my mouth. She apologized over and over while I swallowed what seemed to be a gallon of water in an attempt to quench the red-hot burn assaulting the inside of my mouth. I told her between gulps I would be fine. But good Lord! How had Brigid managed? How would I manage?

While I was putting out the fire in my mouth, I noticed Anne holding in a giggle. A good sign. I might have done the same in her place. But Matthew stared sullenly down at his plate.

"Matthew, you need to eat your breakfast," Mrs. Medrano said.

"I'm not hungry," he snapped.

"That's no way to act," she said.

He took a bite of his fried eggs, pushed himself away from the table, and ran out of the room and up the stairs.

Mrs. Medrano started after him.

"No," I said. "I'll go see to him."

Anne was sitting very still, one hand clutching the other.

"It will be all right, sweetheart," I said. "I promise it will."

She looked up at me, holding back tears. "Mama used to say that to us," she whimpered.

Mrs. Medrano came over and comforted her.

I was nearly to the stairs when Mr. Jessup appeared at the front door. He said he was ready to take the children to school. I thanked him and he went out to wait at the surrey. I started up the stairs. Matthew's door opened and he rushed past me, a leather book satchel in his hand.

I called his name, but he paid me no mind. In another moment he was sitting in the back seat of the surrey, arms folded tightly, his head turned away from the house.

Mr. Jessup glanced at me, a look of resignation on his face.

Mrs. Medrano brought out Anne. That little girl looked so sad. Mr. Jessup helped her into the surrey, climbed into the driver's seat and snapped the reins. I watched as the surrey made its way down the driveway.

"There is still much sadness in this house," Mrs. Medrano said.

"Has their father said anything to them?" I asked.

Mrs. Medrano said nothing. I saw the downcast expression on her face. There was my answer. Sadly, I was not surprised. Charles was certainly not like my Father. Brigid and I were the daughters he loved.

To Charles, his children were only two more items in his house.

It was clear there was nothing to do but give Matthew and Anne time. I knew well enough that children were in many ways a much hardier lot than some of the rest of us.

Mrs. Medrano and I went back inside the house. As we walked toward the dining room there was another question I had, and I saw no reason to wait now.

"Mrs. Medrano, I need to ask you, is there anything you can tell me about the night my sister died? Something Charles didn't mention?"

She shook her head. "No. Nothing."

"Did you see anything? Hear anything?"

"No," she said and lowered her eyes.

"The children were with you that night."

She looked at me, sadness in her dark eyes. "We were in the front sitting room. They were doing their school lessons. I, I wish Mrs. Preston had stayed with us. If she had not gone out..."

"I know this is difficult. Just one more question. Charles said my sister was in the habit of taking walks in the evening. Was that true?"

"Oh, she liked to take walks. *Sí.* Once in the morning and once in the evening. That was before they came to this house. She would take the children with her sometimes. They liked going to the river." She slowly shook her head. "But they do not go to the river now. I am sorry I cannot be of more help."

"You've been very helpful," I said. My other questions could wait for now.

"There is much work to do," Mrs. Medrano said as we reached the dining room.

"Yes, there is. Please, let me start by helping you clear the dishes."

"No, no. Leave them to me." Then she said that with the children in school until later that afternoon, this would be a good time for me to look over the house.

A very good idea, I thought.

I was already familiar with the dining room, Charles's library and the small tower sitting room on the first floor. There was another small sitting room that sat behind the dining room. It looked as though no one had ever been in it, the furniture never sat on. And behind it, a pantry lined with shelves that held all the fine china, porcelain teapots and silver serving trays. There were also drawers for silverware and linens and tablecloths. Had Brigid wanted all of this?

I crossed the hallway to a set of doors. This room was the one behind Charles's library. I opened the doors to a burgundy-colored parlor that looked to be far longer and wider than my girl's dormitory room at the orphan asylum. Taking a few cautious steps inside I felt as though the room had swallowed me up. A grand piano sat at the other end of the parlor, and two glass chandeliers hung from the high ceiling. Large mirrors hung on the wall opposite the two sets of paired windows. Plush sofas and chairs, each covered in burgundy velvet, furnished the parlor. Three Persian rugs spread across the polished wooden floor.

"Mr. Preston intended to host dances in this room," Mrs. Medrano said, startling me as I had not heard her come in.

"It appears big enough to hold the whole town," I said. Appearance was what was important to Charles, flaunting his wealth, his status, himself.

"What do you think of your sister's portrait?" Mrs. Medrano asked.

"Her portrait?" I turned and saw it there on the wall behind me, hanging above the great marble fireplace. Brigid was so lovely. Her chestnut red hair framed her face. She wore an emerald green gown with lace at the shoulders and around the neck. The artist, whoever it was, had captured her in a serene pose, her face in a light that was almost angelic. But there was something about her eyes.

"When was this done?" I asked.

"A year ago, I think," Mrs. Medrano said.

"She was so beautiful." How I wished I had kept in better touch with her, especially after I had joined the convent.

Mrs. Medrano said, "Maybe it is not my place to say, but she did not want it painted."

I looked over at her. "What do you mean?"

"She say to me it was not necessary. But Mr. Preston, he insisted."

Poor Brigid. What had you seen in Charles?

Stepping closer to the portrait I studied Brigid's eyes. I could see there was a sadness in them, a melancholy. How strange, I thought.

Mrs. Medrano asked me if I wanted to see the rest of the house. I told her I would, very much.

We started up the stairs and I mentioned that I had heard strange sounds during the night. "It sounded like someone was crying."

Mrs. Medrano shook her head. "Maybe a fox. I have heard them make sounds like a baby crying."

"Perhaps," I said, "but I've heard foxes, too, and this sounded different."

"One of our neighbors, Mr. Staab, his children have a cat, I think. Maybe it got out. Maybe a coyote caught it."

"What are coyotes? Some kind of dog?"

"It is a cousin of the wolf."

"Well, what I heard didn't sound like any kind of howling a wolf makes. I hope the children didn't lose their cat. You didn't hear that crying last night, did you?"

"I heard nothing."

"This sounded so pitiful."

"Maybe it was a rabbit," she said abruptly. "Rabbits cry like that if they are caught by the coyotes."

Taken aback by her agitation, I asked if I had upset her.

"No," she said, calming herself. "Just coyotes scare me a little."

# Chapter Thirteen

atthew's room and Anne's room were very much like mine. Drapes, fireplace, large bed, armoire and the rest. Anne's room was tidy. She had made her bed. Her toys and dolls sat on the shelves. A beautiful dollhouse stood on a table by the window. Mrs. Medrano said my sister had gotten Anne the dollhouse for her seventh birthday. "But she did not spoil the children," she added. "If they wanted a toy, she told them they would have to earn it with chores."

Just as Mother and Father had raised us, I thought, smiling at the fond memory.

Matthew's bed was unmade. His toy soldiers lay scattered about the floor, the clothes I had seen him in yesterday thrown in a corner.

"I straighten his room each morning," Mrs. Medrano said.

Grim was the word for Charles's bedroom. Dark furnishings and a grey stone fireplace left me only wanting to get out.

Entering Brigid's bedroom, the first thing I noticed was the cheerfulness of it. The cream-colored wallpaper was stamped with tiny garlands of pink rosebuds.

"My sister chose the wallpaper, didn't she?"

"She insisted."

Good for you, Brigid.

\* \* \*

I was surprised about the rooms on the third floor. They were all for Brigid's use. Mrs. Medrano told me it was Charles's gift to her.

"Gift?"

"That is all I know."

In the tower room, an easel stood by the window. Blank canvases leaned against a wall. Another room was intended as a sewing room. The one next to it had books stacked on shelves. There were books on countries of the Orient, of South America, of Europe. A mounted globe stood in a corner. Brigid did love to dream of traveling. The other four rooms sat empty.

\* \* \*

A narrow spiral staircase went up to the fourth floor of the tower. From that high vantage point, coupled with windows on each side, I was afforded a nearly unhindered view in every direction. Great billowy white clouds drifted across a crisp blue sky. Mountains and hills rose off in the distances surrounding us while long flat swathes of land stretched out forming a kind of basin. From somewhere up on the big red mountain the silvery river cut a furrow that flowed toward us. The river lay well behind the house as it meandered by on its way down through the town. Breaks in the trees on both sides along the riverbank provided me with a view of more of those squat mud buildings with their flat roofs over on the other side of the river. But there was something strange about them.

"What is that covering the roof tops?" I asked.

"Dirt," Mrs. Medrano said with a shrug.

"But why dirt?"

"For the same reason we build the walls with adobe bricks. Packing the dirt helps to keep the house warm in the winter and cool in the summer."

Dirt on the roof. More proof that this place truly was upside down. Something else occurred to me and I asked Mrs. Medrano if an earthen roof didn't have considerable weight. She said it did.

"But wouldn't that be dangerous?" I asked.

"Not too much," she said and explained that the buildings here were constructed using heavy beams they call *vigas* to support the roofs. "There has not been an accident for many years."

I could not bring myself to pursue her last statement for fear of what she might tell me and changed the subject. The garden. I saw clearly now in the light of day it reached from the rear of the cook's quarters to the river. Charles had said his property backed up to the river though I had wondered at the time if I had heard him correctly.

Mrs. Medrano said the garden was nearly an acre in size. "But it is not finished."

"Not finished?"

"The day Mrs. Preston and the children come here, she went out to walk around it, to see for herself. She was out there a long time. Workmen were getting started on the wall Mr. Preston told them to build. When she come back in, she say she tell the workmen to stop. I asked her why. She say the garden needs to be bigger. More."

"More?"

"*Sí.* Ah, forgive me again for my Spanish. I mean to say yes."

"That's fine. Please, go on."

"*Sí.* Mrs. Preston say maybe two or three acres more."

Astonished, I asked, "How much land does Charles own?"

Mrs. Medrano said his property covered five acres and pointed out the boundaries from landmark to landmark. She started at the end of the driveway and pointed across to a stand of trees near the back of the Staab property. From there it was a straight line all the way down to the river, then along the riverbank to a ragged, dead tree. It was a misshapen thing with only one thick out-thrust bough remaining.

"Do you see where the road bends near that dead tree?" she said. "Follow that road back here past the house and all the way down to the driveway again."

"Good Lord," I whispered. It was close to three times the size of a city block in Pittsburgh.

She said, "When Mr. Preston started building the house, he told the archbishop that Mrs. Preston wanted a garden. Maybe a week later, the archbishop brought cuttings from some of his roses and his grapes and some fruit trees."

"Well, that was very generous of him."

"Mr. Preston told him how much she love roses. That is his garden there."

It had been impossible to ignore as it sat on the other side of the dirt road boundary from us. An *adobe* wall surrounded the archbishop's garden covering its own five acres. Shaped in a long, rough-looking oval, the wall extended from the side of the cathedral, past Charles's property and stopping short of the dead tree and the river, then curving back around again to the cathedral. Pathways wound through the garden amid an abundance of different kinds of flowers including roses and what Mrs. Medrano said were wildflowers. The archbishop grew vegetables. Fruit trees were arranged in rows while shade trees offered an inviting respite. There was also a large pond that he stocked with trout, no less. And walking bridges led to two small islands in the pond.

"He has been working on it for more than thirty years," she said.

"The archbishop even did the, oh, how do you say?" She motioned with her hands.

"You mean the arrangement of the garden?"

"Ah, *sí.*"

"Did he now," I said, surprised.

She said natural springs feed both his garden as well as Brigid's, and that the archbishop helped design the graded waterways that irrigate Brigid's garden. She looked at me and said, "You know that Mr. and Mrs. Preston donated money to help build the cathedral."

"No, I did not."

"Those were good days." She seemed lost in a reverie for a moment. Then she said, "Did I tell you the archbishop has planted many trees around the town? He started, let me think, it must be more than twenty years ago. Each of the trees he planted he grew in his garden. He calls them his gift to Santa Fe."

She could not recall how many of the trees on the *plaza* were his doing. "At least half, I think," she said. He planted others, she went on, along streets in front of homes around the town; cherry trees, pear trees, apple trees, elms, willows and others. A number of them lined Palace Avenue. They were not difficult to see, tall, full trees they were, some of them twice as big as the houses near them.

I admit I was truly awed by the archbishop's resolve to make an oasis of sorts out of this desert.

"You say he did all this himself?" I asked.

"Well, he does have a man come help from time to time. But he loves his garden. He brought seeds all the way from France. Do you see the two saplings there?" She pointed down at the front of the house.

I had not noticed them on my arrival but there they were inside the driveway circle. Their tender leaves were yellowing.

"They are willows," she said. "The archbishop planted those with his own hands, to welcome his new neighbors." She heaved a sigh. "Mrs. Preston only saw them that first day she came here with the children."

On the far side of the archbishop's walled garden, I saw a stone chapel, or at least the back of one. Its jutting Gothic spires and sharp-pitched roof looked out of place here. So many things here were strange. Mrs. Medrano told me it was the chapel of the Sisters of Loretto. I was not familiar with the Order.

Thirty years ago, the archbishop needed schoolteachers, Mrs. Medrano went on, and the sisters came to Santa Fe to teach. She indicated the tall square building sitting next to the chapel. "That is the school where Anne goes. It is called the Academy of Our Lady of Light."

"And where is Matthew's school?" I asked.

"Much further." Turning to the windows facing the back of the house, she pointed. "The long red roof is St. Michael's."

Indeed, it was much further, across the river on a rise. A cross sat atop a white cupola in the center of that red Mansard roof with its dozen windows all in a neat row. St. Michael's had three floors. Mrs. Medrano said the top two floors served as the dormitory as most of the boys boarded there.

"The Christian Brothers teach there," she said. "Many years ago, the archbishop convinced them to come here from France. He has a way of getting what he wants. *Simpático*. Charming. You will see."

"I shall look forward to meeting him."

I also saw what appeared to be a ruin of some kind nestled close beside the school building and asked her about it.

"That is San Miguel chapel," she said.

"Did you say a chapel?"

"*Sí.*"

I looked at it again. Harder this time. It was a square structure made of those *adobe* bricks, though it still bore more resemblance to a great unsteady pile of stones than a house of God. Astonished, I said, "My Lord."

She smiled. "It is very old. It is the first church they built here."

"And when was that?"

"Almost three hundred years ago, I think. The Franciscan friars built it. You can see there at the front of it where the bell tower used to be." The remains of a stunted looking square of bricks on top of the front end of the chapel were visible. She said a terrible storm had passed through town, so strong it toppled the tower, sending it and the large bell crashing to the ground.

"The bell was *muy bonita.* Very beautiful." It was cast in Spain, she said, over five centuries ago when the Spanish were fighting to drive the Moors from their country. The Spaniards fought and lost every battle and they prayed to St. Joseph for help. So desperate was their situation and so devout was their faith, they vowed to cast a bell as a sign of their confidence that he would aid them in their fight.

"The people brought plates and cups made of gold and silver and copper to be melted down," she went on. "Women gave up their rings, their bracelets, everything. When they cast the bell, they put an inscription on it. *San José ruega por nosotros.* It means Saint Joseph pray for us. And August 9, 1356. That was the date it was cast. It is said from the very first time they rang the bell, the Spanish army rode from victory to victory. Many years later, the friars brought it with them here when they came to bring God's word to Mexico."

She turned away from the window. "I remember the first time I hear the bell as a child. It was like the angels singing."

"How beautiful. And where is the bell now?"

"At the chapel. It sings no more."

"I'm sorry. The storm must have been very bad. When did it happen?"

She thought a moment. "Maybe twelve years ago."

"Did you say twelve years?"

"*Sí.* It is very heavy, the bell."

I stood there trying to find the words. How could such a thing be? They leave a church bell on the ground for twelve years. It was one more strange thing about this bewildering, upside down place.

"Maybe you would like to see the garden now?" Mrs. Medrano said.

"Yes, I think so," I said. A walk through Brigid's garden was what I needed.

## Chapter Fourteen

We returned downstairs and Mrs. Medrano led me to the back porch. I asked her if she would care to accompany me, but she had housekeeping chores to attend to and needed to get started. Reaching into a side closet, she took out an umbrella and handed it to me. I took it, for the sun was already bright in the sky.

She said, "I hope you will find the garden to your liking. Mrs. Preston, she wanted it to be a special place."

Stepping out onto the covered porch, the air was crisp, but I felt no need for a coat. I heard the sharp crack of wood and saw Mr. Jessup over by the stable splitting short logs. A goodly pile already lay stacked against the stable wall.

Gathering the split pieces into the crook of his arm, he caught sight of me.

I opened the umbrella and tipped it toward him. "For the sun," I called out.

"Yes, ma'am. And remember, the air is thinner up this high." He nodded and went back to his chore.

The garden lay a few yards before me. The first thing I noticed was an unfinished arched gateway and the beginnings of a wall, both using the same red brick as the house. A considerable amount of those bricks stood stacked in several large squares just behind the cook's quarters. A trench for the wall had been started too, or at least the remnants of one, intended to enclose the entire garden. I had no doubt that Charles would eventually get around to having the wall finished one day. Order was a rigid obsession of his, after all.

Stepping into the garden, I discovered a wide gravel path wound through the sea of colors Brigid's garden still held.

The first of Brigid's rose beds were laid out in long rows, and others arranged in ovals. Almost every bed still held their blooms of yellow, red, pink, orange, and white. I bent down at the first bed I came to, put my face close to the red bloom and drew in the sweet pungent fragrance. They were beautiful, and the thorns sharp.

I was unfamiliar with many of the flowers. Some edged the pathway while others grew in their own beds. A string of delicate orange buds decorated stringy yet graceful plants. Another had thick bunches of blue and white flowers shaped like conch shells. Still others burst forth in glorious bright lavender-colored buds. A sturdy big yellow flower with a black center sprouted up in large patches. Seeing them I could not help but smile. Orange trumpets climbed several wooden lattices that had been placed along little side paths.

Green shrubs were scattered about, but not in any haphazard fashion. Their placement seemed designed to give borders to the splashes of color.

Bunches of light-yellow colored grapes—Malaga grapes, Mrs. Medrano said they were—hung temptingly from two grape arbors placed on opposite sides of the garden. These were the grapes the archbishop had brought over. Admiring several delectable bunches, I nearly tripped over one of the graded waterways lined with grey rock.

In the center of the garden stood the trellis supporting a variety of climbing roses in colors of scarlet and pink. Two benches sat beneath the trellis. Mrs. Medrano had told me my sister thought it a most tranquil spot. Even with the sound of Mr. Jessup's wood chopping, the garden was a peaceful place. I could easily spend countless hours here. I wished Brigid could have.

Suddenly, I felt the need to sit down, a giddy sensation overtaking me. Now I understood about that thin air Mr. Jessup mentioned. After a few minutes of fanning myself with my hand and some good deep breaths, my head seemed clearer, my balance reclaimed. I got to my feet and continued along the garden path.

Hardy cottonwood trees and brushy cedars stood near the outer edges of the garden offering shade. The cedar trees possessed green bunches of scaly leaves and smoky-blue colored berries. Their gray sinewy trunks and branches make these trees look as old as the Commandments themselves.

Almost a dozen fruit trees, their leaves turning, had been planted toward the end of the garden, all young and barely as tall as myself. I could not tell the difference from one tree to the other, neither apricot nor cherry nor apple. Would I be here long enough to see their blossoms or taste their fruit? I wondered.

I glanced toward the archbishop's garden. The walls were high enough to hinder any would-be thieves from climbing over to steal anything. All the more reason Charles would have the wall put around Brigid's garden.

But as to the archbishop's garden, I admit I hoped to have a closer look at it one day soon. Perhaps Mrs. Medrano would introduce me to the archbishop after Mass this Sunday.

Overhead I heard the deep gurgling croak of ravens. Several of the black-winged scavengers circled lazily above the garden and then drifted off toward the red mountains.

It was a few yards from the end of the garden to the river. Cottonwoods grew along its banks. Strong tall trees with a thick corky bark, their shiny leaves had begun to turn revealing a palette of yellows and golds. I was familiar with cottonwoods as they had a vast population around Pittsburgh, too. In the early summer their white fluffy lint drifted over the city like so much snow.

But there was that dead tree by the river Mrs. Medrano had pointed out as a marker on Charles's property. Maybe twenty feet tall, it stood grey and gnarled with its one thick, ragged bough jutting up at the sky. Like the tree Judas Iscariot hanged himself from. Looking at it, I suddenly felt cold.

Turning away, I closed my umbrella and approached the sandy riverbank where sunlight peaked through the tree branches and danced upon the gentle waters, clean and clear, shimmering invitingly. It was not a wide river, only three or four yards from bank to bank. Peering more closely I caught a glimpse of scattered river rock and heard the ripples speaking in soft whispers.

My heart heaved and I brushed away a tear, for Mrs. Medrano had said it was here on this embankment that poor Brigid met her awful fate. So strange that such a tragedy could have happened in this serene place. I would see the local constabulary about their investigation soon.

The sound of Mr. Jessup's chopping had ceased. I looked back toward the house but saw no sign of him.

I heard a child's laugh. On the other side of the river was a woman with a little girl. They were coming down a worn pathway. Chickens pecked at the rutted ground. A goat chewed on few blades of tall grass sprouting up at the corner of a dismal mud shanty. The child had long black hair and a cherub's face. She wore a simple white garment. Her mother was dressed in what had to be a long brown blanket. It was looped over one shoulder then around under the other and fastened on one side with a large shiny pin. She, too, had a round face but her black hair was in a long braid.

The little girl was nearly to the water's edge when her mother said something that halted the girl in her place. The girl turned, her back to me now. Her mother bent down, spoke to the child who squealed with pleasure and splashed into the river up to her knees.

A smile crept over my face. That young mother saw me and straightened up, as though trying to discern my intentions. I nodded and she slowly returned my nod.

The cottonwood leaves rustled above me. It was such a soothing sound and from only a touch of breeze. Almost instantly the leaves grew still, and I felt the breeze die.

Across the river, the mother stared at me, a stark expression on her face. Making the sign of the cross, she snatched her child from the water and hurried away.

I raised my hand and opened my mouth to call her back, but she had already disappeared around a mud building. The goat and the chickens had fled, as well.

An unsettling disquiet enveloped me, like something was closing in behind me. My body tensed; my heart pounded. I took a deep breath and a firm grip on the umbrella handle, preparing myself to wallop any lout who might be attempting to sneak up on me. I spun around. No one was there. Only the garden stood before me, and the house beyond.

I let out a long breath and a shrill squawk made me jump. Turning, I saw it, a large black raven roosting on a low nearby cottonwood branch. It leaned forward and squawked at me three times in an insolent manner. Cocking its black head to one side, it fixed its shiny dark eye on me, looking up and down as though taking the measure of me. I was about to swing my umbrella at it for scaring me so when it ruffled its coal black plumage, tilted its head back and loosed a series of deep rasping croaks, taunting and cold. Spreading its wings, it flew up over the trees and out of sight.

I drew a deep breath and touched my face. It felt flushed and hot. I heard voices. Looking down the river, I saw two young men sitting on the far bank lazily tossing pebbles into the water. Calm as prayers things were, but not me. I felt strangely lightheaded.

"Ma'am?" the voice said.

Startled I was, and saw it was Mr. Jessup.

"Is everything all right?" he asked.

Flustered, I said, "Yes, I'm fine. How, how long have you been there?"

"Just now. I heard that raven giving you about eight kinds of grief."

"Oh. Yes," I said, trying to calm myself.

Mr. Jessup tilted his head up at the sky. "Odd about that raven. Taking a dislike to you that way. And you doing nothing to provoke it."

There was something familiar about this. Nothing to provoke it. I had heard that before. Yes. The train conductor said the same thing to me at Las Vegas when the raven flew at me. But that was silly. It means nothing. A strange coincidence was all.

"I think I'll go to the house now," I said. I managed to slide the umbrella open, and we started back. Walking quickly made me feel a little less anxious. I asked Mr. Jessup if he knew who the people were that lived on the other side of the river.

"Poor Mexes and Indians mostly. Servants and bricklayers and such."

"I see."

"Ma'am, are you certain you're all right?"

"Why do you ask?"

"Well, because you're acting kind of fidgety, if you'll pardon my saying. Did somebody back there say or try to do something to you, ma'am?"

"No, no, nothing of the kind." We stopped under the trellis, and I told him of the incident with the mother and her child suddenly running away, though I made no mention of the queer feeling of something lurking behind me.

"Sounds like it was an Indian woman," he said. "I wouldn't take anything they do to heart. Indians have their own ways."

"But why would she take her child and go like that?"

"Maybe on account of you being a stranger to her. They're a superstitious lot."

"Superstitious? Of what?"

He chuckled. "For one, they prize a little bird in these parts that's got long legs. I forget what they call it."

"I don't understand. What's so special about this bird?"

"They say it can outrun a man."

I stared at him a moment. "Are you making this up, Mr. Jessup?"

"I'm telling you the honest truth, ma'am. They believe this bird can ward off evil spirits. Maybe it chases them away." He grunted and rubbed his moustache. "Wait one now. Did you say that Indian woman crossed herself?"

"That she did."

"That's it then."

"What is?"

"Christian Indians. Worst kind of Indian to my way of thinking."

"Mr. Jessup, we are all God's children."

"Ma'am, they may have been baptized and go to church and believe in Jesus, but the way I hear it, they haven't given up their Indian ways."

"And what ways are those?"

"Everything means something to an Indian. When the wind

blows or rain falls it's more than wind blowing or rain coming down. Blowing wind is the Great Spirit talking to them. And rain falling has a, well, I don't recall now, but it has some kind of meaning. Even a high place, like a mountain, is important to them. They see things where we don't. Everything tells them something. I ask you, what kind of religion is that?"

Mr. Jessup kept talking but I was not listening. Had that Indian woman seen something I had not? No. What a preposterous thought. How could she have? Were my imaginings real? Of course not. Ludicrous is what it was.

# Chapter Fifteen

eaching the house, I set the umbrella back in the side closet and called out to Mrs. Medrano. She did not answer. Going into the main foyer I called her name again.

"Here, Miss Danaher," she said from somewhere above me. A moment later she appeared over the staircase railing on the second floor. She held a feather duster in her hand.

Not wanting to keep her from her house chores, I said I was coming up to see her. Climbing the stairs, I stopped part way up feeling lightheaded once again. Taking a couple of deep breaths, my dizziness went away, and I proceeded to Brigid's room where Mrs. Medrano was finishing her cleaning. She said she had already seen to Charles's room, as well as Anne's, Matthew's, and my room. "I clean and dust Mrs. Preston's room every week, too. She was. . . She liked to have a clean house."

That was our Mother's doing. She saw to it Brigid and I were well versed in cleanliness. A clean home and a clean conscience go hand in hand, she would say. She also said that no daughter of hers would ever be mistaken for a street urchin in ragged clothes. In that regard, I was in need of some assistance in my own right this day.

"I could use your help, Mrs. Medrano. As I have no idea how long I may be here, and all I have is the dress I'm wearing and it could stand a good washing, I think it would be best if I had another.

Could you tell me where I would go to purchase an everyday dress?"

"Mr. Preston has an account at Mr. Spiegelberg's store," she said. "That is where Mrs. Preston bought her dresses."

I remembered the name. "Then that is where I shall have to go. Mr. Jessup said he could take me after he finishes his chores. I also asked him to take me to the cemetery. I want to see my sister's grave."

"Maybe you would like to take some roses to her."

"An excellent idea. Thank you."

"She will like those. She liked the simple things." A look came over her face and she wagged her finger in the air. "I just thought of something."

She opened Brigid's armoire. I knew I could not possibly fit into one of Brigid's dresses as she was a wisp compared to me. I started to say as much but before I could finish, Mrs. Medrano had reached up to a top shelf and pulled down a hat.

"Mrs. Preston wore this when she was going into town during the day," she said holding the hat out to me.

I took it from her. It was a soft brown felt hat with a good wide brim. Very plain.

"Mr. Preston hated it when she went out in it," Mrs. Medrano said. "He told her it made her look like kitchen help."

Yet another reason to dislike Charles immensely. I put the hat on and was pleased to find it fit.

"This will do nicely," I said and took it off.

"He bought her other hats, very fancy, but she would not wear them," Mrs. Medrano went on. "She did not like to look proud."

I peered into the armoire. There were five simple dresses, and two lovely dresses with lace trimmings. One of those pretty dresses was light blue and the other was the emerald green one Brigid wore in her portrait.

"Mrs. Preston picked out the dresses herself," Mrs. Medrano said, taking her hand and smoothing out a fold on the green lacy dress. "She would only wear the very pretty ones on special occasions, like Christmas Day and Easter Sunday." She sighed. "And to dinners at the Governor's Residence."

"The governor invited them to dinner?"

"Over the last three or maybe four years they went a few times."

"Do you know why they were invited?"

"I think it had to do with Mr. Catron," she said. "Mrs. Preston told me they would see him and his wife there, too. And some other lawyers."

"I had no idea," I said. I had noticed Mrs. Medrano lower her eyes when she mentioned Mr. Catron's name.

"Well," she said, "Mrs. Preston never liked to go to those dinners."

"Did she say why?"

She shrugged. "I think she was more comfortable wearing her hat."

We looked at each other and could not help ourselves. We burst out laughing like school children.

Calming ourselves, Mrs. Medrano said, "I think your sister would be very pleased if you wore her hat during your stay."

There was something in Mrs. Medrano's voice when she said it, a feeling. Perhaps it was pride. Perhaps tenderness.

I said, "You took good care of my sister, didn't you?"

She nodded. "I liked her very much." She seemed lost in her thoughts for a moment and then she quickly recovered and said she would ask Mr. Jessup to get the surrey ready to take me to town. "And while he is doing that, I can make you some coffee, if you would like."

"Only if you will join me."

She smiled, nodded and started to the door. "Did you enjoy the garden?"

"It's beautiful." I glanced out the window for another look and gasped. A winding swath of death had descended over the garden. Flowers were dying before my eyes. Green leaves turned brown and brittle. Rose petals shriveled up black. How could it be? And I remembered. This black path, the way it wheeled over the garden, was the same ground I had watched that shadow cover last night!

"Mrs. Medrano!" I called, still staring out the window.

I heard her coming up behind me. "Is something wrong?"

I stepped away from the widow. "Look down there, in the garden."

She peered out the window, moving her head from side to side.

"What is it?" she asked.

"Don't you see it?"

"I do not see anything."

Impossible! I spun around to the window.

"You don't see that black—" My words caught in my throat. The garden bloomed. The dead swath was gone.

## Chapter Sixteen

"The thin air here can play tricks on you when you are not used to it," Mrs. Medrano said, placing a cup of coffee and a napkin on the small table next to me.

I thanked her and could not help thinking that perhaps both the sun and air here were unforgiving. They had to be the culprits. What else could possibly explain it? Perplexing as it was, I tried to console myself that I need not feel so foolish for seeing things that weren't really there. Otherwise, I might have thought I was losing my mind, God help me.

We were in the tower sitting room. Mrs. Medrano sat in a green velvet covered chair across from me, holding her cup in her lap. "Please, try the coffee. I hope it is not too strong for you," she said.

Lifting the cup to my mouth I sampled a taste. Indeed, it was strong yet soothing. She had cut the bitterness by flavoring it with something delightfully sweet. I asked her what it was, and she replied she had added a teaspoon of sugar and a quarter spoonful of cinnamon. That was easy enough to remember. Perhaps when I returned to the convent I could convince Mother Superior that such an indulgence could be made for the sisters on special days, such as Christmas and Easter Sunday.

"Mrs. Preston always had a cup of my coffee in the morning," she said with a contented smile.

I took another sip and savored the intoxicating aroma rising up out of my cup. Glancing at the grandfather clock I saw it was nearly a quarter to eleven.

Mr. Jessup was out in the stable hitching the team of horses to the surrey to take me into town. He had unhitched them after taking the children to school believing he would not be going out again until much later that afternoon. It was no trouble, he said.

Holding the cup in both my hands, I settled back into my chair, happy for this intermission to speak some more with Mrs. Medrano. I felt quite comfortable with her already, a friendship on the cusp. I asked her when she had first come to work for Brigid and my brother-in-law.

"It was less than a year after Mrs. Preston had Matthew," she said. "She was glad for the help. Matthew was a handful."

"At least there was plenty of room."

A puzzled look crossed her face. "No. Only two rooms," she said.

"But I thought Mr. Jessup told me that before Charles built this house he and my sister lived in a house in town on, oh, what was it? Jackson Street?"

"That was Johnson Street. Six rooms. But that was not the first place they lived." She said when Brigid and Charles first got to Santa Fe, they rented the two cramped rooms down on Sandoval Street. "It was all they could afford. Mr. Preston hired me after he became a lawyer, and that was a few months before they moved to the house on Johnson Street."

"That first place must have been a snug fit," I said.

"Oh, very much."

"Did my sister tell you that we lived in a small three-room house in Pittsburgh?"

"She did," she said with a smile. "She told me you both slept in the same bed, and your father, he would tell you frightening stories at night."

"She told you about that?" I laughed. "Coming here and living in those little rooms didn't bother her, then. What about Mr. Preston? How did he like it?"

Her grin disappeared. "He did not."

That came as no surprise to me. "What did he object to?" I asked, savoring another sip of the coffee.

"Many things. An old man named Lopez had a store across the street where he sold stoves. He would set them outside for people to see. Mr. Preston did not like looking at them."

Charles was a snobbish one even then. I lowered my cup and brought a napkin to my lip to catch an errant drop of coffee.

"And he always had to duck his head coming through the front doorway," she went on. "The doorway was low, and he would bump his head hard if he was not careful. But I think mostly he did not like it because of the blood."

"Did you say blood?"

She nodded. "It had a dirt floor. Many places here do. We pour pig's blood on the dirt. Would you like some more coffee?"

I did, but this new revelation had given me pause and I politely shook my head. Good Lord! First dirt on rooftops and now bloody dirt floors. I was almost afraid to ask, but I did. "Why would you do that now? With the blood, I mean."

"To harden the dirt. The home my husband and I had when he was alive had a dirt floor. We poured pig's blood on it and once it has dried it is hard as a stone. We covered it with rugs. I remember Mrs. Preston say she thought it was very clever."

That was proof enough that Brigid was more accepting of the upside-down ways here than I was. And yet, I had to admit this blood

103

business held a certain ghastly appeal, like something from a bedtime story Father would tell. "And what about Mr. Preston?"

She set her coffee cup down and shook her head emphatically. "He did not think it was clever. He always say he would have a house with a wooden floor and big doors someday. A proper house, he called it."

"Did my sister want this house?"

She sighed. "She wanted what her husband wanted."

That could mean yes, and might also mean no.

"Yes, I understand," I said, "but what did she think of this house when she saw it that day?"

"Oh, it was like a palace. So many rooms and so many floors. But the garden." She spread her hands apart. "She told me it was like something from a fairy tale."

I suppose I would have as well, had it been me, but then my dream would not have included Charles. Mother told both Brigid and me on more than one occasion, mind you, that she had fallen in love with Father the moment she first laid eyes on him. She said she knew right then he was the man she would marry. What I gathered from my Mother was that people have little control over the urges of the heart. I had promised my whole life and all my love to Christ when I joined the convent. But, God help me please, what did Brigid see in Charles?

"Mrs. Medrano, was my sister happy?"

She hesitated, then said, "Of course. She loved her children. She, she loved living here, in Santa Fe. The people, she liked them very much. The archbishop. Mr. Spiegelberg. So many people. And they liked her, too. *Sí*. Very happy."

She had not mentioned Charles. Something was not right. I could feel it.

"I've been wondering," I said. "That day my sister and the children came to the house for the first time, Charles told me he had to leave for Denver. Do you know what the business was he had there?"

"Only that he was going to Denver. Mr. Preston never tell us anything about his work. Mr. Catron, he sent a telegram to Mr. Preston's hotel the next morning telling him to come back right away."

"How many days does it take the train to get to Denver?"

"Two days, I think. I remember him saying he has to change trains. He came back five, no six days later."

Perhaps there had been delays. For the time being, I chose to believe that.

I spoke gently to Mrs. Medrano. "I don't mean to upset you, but did you see my sister that night after she was attacked?"

She shook her head sadly. "The doctor say she must go to the hospital right away. I kept the children with me in the house."

"Has there been any word from the chief of police?"

"Nothing I know of."

"Has Charles gone to see him, then?"

"I wish I could say yes," she said, clutching the napkin in her hand. "I do not think so. But he never say anything about it."

That man was so frustrating! Did he even care?

I hated to think of the next question but considering Charles's cavalier handling of things as I saw it, it was a question that needed asking. "Charles did take Matthew and Anne to see their mother in the hospital, didn't he?"

"*Sí*. Once. It was very upsetting for them and they did not want to go back. But they ask every day when their *mamá* was coming home." She cast her eyes down. "They could not stop crying at her funeral. Such a sad day. It is still hard to believe it was only two weeks ago."

The sound of the front door opening was followed by heavy

footsteps in the foyer. Mr. Jessup appeared in the doorway of the sitting room, his big sombrero in his hand.

"Ready to take you to town when you are, ma'am," he said.

## Chapter Seventeen

We drove down Palace Avenue toward the *plaza*. On my head was Brigid's hat and, in my hand, I carried a small bouquet of red roses wrapped in paper that I had snipped from her garden. Mr. Jessup said the hat suited me and my sister would like it that I brought her flowers.

Passing St. Vincent's Hospital, I thought of asking Mr. Jessup if he knew how often my brother-in-law had gone to visit Brigid while she was being cared for there. But I already knew the answer.

Reaching the *plaza*, Mr. Jessup turned onto Washington Avenue, moving toward the north edge of town. Soon we passed the last buildings on that avenue and the dusty road curved down and angled away from town in the direction of scrub-covered rolling hills and a large lonely-looking walled square about a quarter mile distant.

Mr. Jessup looked back over his shoulder and said, "Rosario Cemetery up ahead, ma'am."

A copse of cedars crowded near the entrance. The wall was tall and made of those *adobe* bricks. A box-shaped building with a cross on top of it sat inside the walls. Mr. Jessup said it was the chapel.

Scattered outside the cemetery walls were a few cottonwood trees outnumbered by more cedars. Even fewer trees were in evidence inside the cemetery.

Drawing closer, I saw something lying in the road. A small carcass, grey and headless. Flies swarmed and buzzed over it.

"Looks like ravens already picked over that old rabbit," Mr. Jessup said.

"Is that what it was?"

He nodded. "The coyote catches the rabbit and I suspect something bigger, likely a mountain lion came along and scared off the coyote who dropped that rabbit and ran. The lion probably caught the coyote. That's the way of things out here."

A young boy tended goats grazing near the narrow gate where we pulled to a halt. He began singing in Spanish, a melancholy tune it was. He tapped his staff to the ground and herded the goats on.

For reasons I could not explain, I was suddenly hesitant to walk through that arched gate. I wanted to see my sister's final resting place. Yet, something held me fast to that spot. Was it a reluctance to face the finality of Brigid's passing? Or was it guilt on my part that I thought I had somehow not been a good sister to her?

Whatever the reason for my apprehension, my heart pounded, and I felt jittery and blurted out a question to Mr. Jessup about other cemeteries in town. He said there was another Catholic cemetery on the other side of the river and one next to the cathedral. "Both of them got filled up a while back. Plenty of room here, though."

"And where are the others buried, those not of the Catholic faith?"

"Well, the Masons, they've been operating one, oh, some thirty years now, or so I've been told. And new one called Fairview. Nobody I know of has been buried there yet."

Mr. Jessup pushed open the wrought iron gate. The hinges groaned. Two rabbits darted out in different directions from behind a nearby headstone.

Clutching the roses in my hand, I took hold of my nerves, asked God for strength, and stepped through the gate. Perhaps it was

God's grace, or maybe Brigid had placed her calming hand upon my shoulder, but my anxiousness slowly subsided.

The cemetery was divided into three sections, each separated from the others by low walls. The largest section, a military cemetery Mr. Jessup said it was, lay off to the far left side. It took up at least half of the grounds. Headstones in three neat, long rows stood white in the bright sun.

The remainder of the cemetery was divided in half again. Mr. Jessup did not know why it had been sectioned off in that fashion. One part stretched up the hillside. Tombstones and crosses lay scattered over it.

The small chapel overlooked the other part of the cemetery. Brigid's grave lay near the chapel. Mr. Jessup took me along the worn hard pathway where grave markers stood, some inscribed with Spanish names and others with English names. But I also saw a few Italian names, and French, as well. I asked Mr. Jessup about them. He said the archbishop needed stone masons for work on the cathedral.

"Apparently, greasers got no talent for carving stone," he said. "The archbishop, he sent word out and a couple dozen stone masons came over from Europe." He chuckled. "There was a party of frog-eaters that got lost coming across Texas. They showed up here about three months late. Said they knew when their time comes to die, they would not go to hell because they had already been to Texas."

I had no need to ask Mr. Jessup the meaning of frog-eaters. It was a term my Father used on more than a few occasions in jokes and stories I had overheard him tell his friends about the French.

The sharp sound of a shovel digging into earth drew my attention. On the other side of a cedar tree were two gravediggers performing their duty. One grave was already dug, though it was small, as though for a child's coffin. Another was being dug. It, too, looked like a child's grave. One digger leaned on his shovel, saw me, straightened up and nodded his head.

Closer to the chapel, simple wooden crosses marked other graves. Some had names of those who had joined the religious life and listed only the year of their death. Sister Xavier, 1870. Brother Isfrid, 1874. Brother Gelatian, 1882.

Mr. Jessup led me to the spot where a marked grave stood off by itself.

"I'll be over here, ma'am," he said and moved away to give me time alone with my sister.

The sound of the gravedigger's shoveling seemed a strange distant echo now as I walked toward the grave. It was as though the whole world had gone silent. My knees weakened. I made myself go on. The simple headstone read:

BRIGID PRESTON

BELOVED WIFE AND MOTHER

BORN MAY 10, 1857

DIED SEPTEMBER 18, 1883

Carved above her name were two angels facing each other, hands clasped in prayer.

Tears ran down my cheeks. Wiping them away, I knelt down on the hard ground and laid the roses in front of the headstone. After making the sign of the cross I said a prayer, asking God in His tender mercy to take my sister into the care and comfort of His arms. My mind became a jumble of thoughts. So many things I wished I had told Brigid. Things I should have said.

I drew a ragged breath.

*Dearest Brigid*, my thoughts began, *Father went to the Lord first, and Mother followed. I always knew they would go before us. That's the way of things, how they are supposed to be. Our parents raised us, tried to show us how to be decent, respectful girls. Remember what Mother used to say to us? Tell the truth, shame the devils, and use the brains God gave you. You should still be here teaching your own children those very things. And telling them the bedtime stories Father used to scare us with. Your whole life lay ahead of you. Watching your children grow up and live their own lives. Charles is. . . Well, I don't want to say anything about Charles here. It would only upset you.*

I turned Charles from my thoughts and again to my sister.

*You know, I wish I could have told you about my orphan girls. Many a night they begged me to tell them a ghostly Irish tale. My girls. They would have made you laugh. But now, I'll never hear your laugh again, or see your sweet face in this life.*

I gently ran my fingertips over her name. The stone was cold and hard. Cold and hard. Those were three words that would never have occurred to me when I thought of my sister.

My heart swelled. I closed my eyes and made a solemn vow to Brigid. *I have no idea how long I will be here, but God helping me, I shall do all in my power to take good care of young Matthew and Anne for as long as need be. Danaher blood runs in them. My orphan girls will have to wait. Matthew and Anne need me more.*

"A lot of folks came to your sister's funeral," Mr. Jessup said as I got to my feet and brushed the dirt from my dress.

"I'm glad," I said. "A fine thing."

He said the archbishop himself gave the service, saying the funeral Mass for her in the cathedral. "It was full, every seat. Over a thousand people. Some were standing outside the doors because there wasn't enough room for everybody to sit."

"I wished I could have been here," I said as we started walking back down the path. The gravediggers had completed their tasks and sat in the shade of the cedar tree.

"After the Mass everybody followed the hearse here," Mr. Jessup went on. "Longest line of carriages I have ever seen for a burial. Mr. Catron was there with his wife, and Mr. Spiegelberg and his brothers and their families. The governor came. Doc Symington. Mr. and Mrs. Staab. A lot of folks."

I caught sight of a flatbed wagon pulled by a horse coming up the road from the opposite direction we had taken. Two small coffins lay side by side on the bed. A dozen or so people followed it on foot dressed in black, led by a balding priest wearing a white alb over his black cassock. Behind him, two men supported a woman, hands at her elbows. A black veil covered her face. I could hear her sobs.

Mr. Jessup and I had climbed into the surrey as the sad little party reached the cemetery gates. Their black clothes were dusty from their trek. I asked Mr. Jessup to wait to leave until the mourners had passed.

Several men came forward and pulled the small coffins from the wagon bed. The procession started through the gates.

I heard the veiled woman cry out something in Spanish as she nearly fell to her knees, the men catching her.

After they had gone inside, I asked Mr. Jessup if he knew what the woman was saying.

He looked back over his shoulder. "She said, 'My children.'" He told me there was a story in the newspaper the day before about a couple of children who had fallen into the river and drowned. "That's them, I'd say."

I made the sign of the cross and offered a silent prayer for their souls and for their mother.

Mr. Jessup held the reins and asked, "Where to next, ma'am?"

\*    \*    \*

The door of the office of the chief of police stood open. Inside I saw a thin-faced man with bushy eyebrows sitting behind a desk, a badge pinned to his shirt. He paid me no mind, transfixed as he was reading the book he held in his hands. Drawing closer, I recognized the cover of the volume as Mr. Fairchild's lurid epic with the unfortunate Constance Wiley menaced by the looming black shade.

"Excuse me," I said.

He snapped his head up at me, startled, a flush of red coloring his cheeks. "Begging your pardon, miss," he said, as he stood up, his chair scraping the floor behind him. "Can I help you?"

I asked him if he was the chief of police.

He chuckled and said he was not then told me that Chief Chavez was over at the courthouse. When I asked if he was expected to return soon, the officer said he could not say with any certainty. "The chief is a witness in a case. All depends on when he gets called to testify. You ask me, Saw Dust Charlie tried robbing the wrong store."

"Oh?"

"I guess you must not be from around here," he said, scratching the back of his head.

"No, I'm not."

"It's a big case. That store old Charlie and his gang broke into, the chief is part owner. He happened to be going by it late that night and saw a light where it shouldn't have been. Caught Charlie and Dave Cobb and Woodrow McCord coming out the back, their arms loaded down and a stolen horse and wagon waiting. He had to shoot Dave Cobb when he went for his gun. The chief's store was the third place Charlie and his boys had broken into in a week. The newspaper called the chief's action highly commendable."

113

"I see," I said. "And what about the sheriff?"

"Paper ain't mentioned the sheriff for a while."

"I meant do you know where the sheriff might be?"

"More than likely at the jail, I expect." He raised his arm and pointed, indicating the direction. "Down the street a ways. You'll see the sign. Or ask anybody."

# Chapter Eighteen

The squat brown building housing the jail was located on Water Street near the corner of Bridge Street. People said it got the name of Water Street because when heavy rains came, the Santa Fe River often overflowed its banks and flooded this road, but at this moment Water Street was as dry and coarse as every other avenue in town.

A fellow with a hammer was up on a ladder by the doorway of the jail. He was pounding nails into the cracked wall to hold a new sign in place that said JAIL. Pulling to a stop near the door, Mr. Jessup called out to the fellow as he climbed down the ladder. "Say deputy, is the sheriff inside?"

The deputy glanced over, a sour expression on his leathery face. He nodded and taking the ladder, headed up the street away from us for perhaps some further work to perform.

"He's a surly one," I heard Mr. Jessup say under his breath.

Alighting from the surrey I said, "I don't know how long I'll be. Not too long, I should think."

Entering the jail office, I heard a strange noise. It sounded like a rooster crowing, but not a real rooster. More like someone trying to imitate one. It came from behind a heavy-looking door across the room.

A lanky man stood before a desk with his back to me. I recognized the checkered trousers the man wore as belonging to Mr. Fairchild. His clothes were rumpled and dirty. He suddenly jumped, as did I, on hearing a loud angry rant of Spanish words. Abruptly the crowing stopped.

The speaker of Spanish was sitting behind the desk. He had not noticed me, but I could see he had big shoulders and slicked down black hair.

"Now you listen close, mister book writer," I heard him say. "I will not tolerate public drunkenness in this town. You do it again, I guarantee your sentence will be considerably longer and less comfortable." He reached down and brought up Mr. Fairchild's scuffed valise and put it on top of his desk. "The train leaves today at five o'clock. You be on it."

"Yes, sir, sheriff," Mr. Fairchild said, his voice weak.

"What time did I say that train leaves?"

"Five o'clock."

"Go on. Get out of here."

Taking his valise, Mr. Fairchild turned and seeing me, dropped the valise. Out spilled copies of his slender novel about red horror on the black mesa. He bent down to gather up his belongings. His face was covered with a scruffy two-day growth of beard, and I could tell he recognized me.

I stooped to help him. Oh, the odor of the man! Stale sweat and whiskey. Reaching for a few loose copies, I heard something. A whisper.

"Pardon me?" I asked low.

He hurriedly scooped the last copies of his book into the valise, his eyes averted from me.

"Mr. Fairchild?" I whispered.

Snatching the copies of his book from my hand, he mumbled a thank you then ducked his head and hurried away.

I was certain I had heard him say the words. They sounded so clear, yet so strange: "Beware the river."

Perplexed, I decided my ears must have played a trick on me. Only a few moments ago I had been greeted by the sound of a rooster crowing, or something crowing. Straightening up, I faced the man behind the desk.

"State your business, miss," he said, frowning.

A side door opened, and a red headed fellow came in, papers in his hand. Younger than the other man, he had smallpox scars covering his face. He wore a white shirt and stringy black tie. A shiny badge was fastened to his black vest.

"I'm looking for Sheriff Martínez," I said.

"That would be me," the broad-shouldered man said. Like Mrs. Medrano, the sheriff's skin was coppery in color. He had a doughy face and a thick moustache.

Crossing the floor I said, "I'm Catherine Danaher. Brigid Preston was my sister."

"Sheriff Romulo Martínez," he said, his frown disappearing as he stood up from behind his desk. "My condolences, Miss Danaher."

He, too, wore a white shirt with a black sting tie and a badge. I decided it was likely a uniform of sorts for the sheriff and his deputies. The buttons of Sheriff Martínez's shirt strained against his big belly.

"Thank you" I said. "I would like to ask about any progress on my sister's case."

"*Sí*. Of course." He looked over at the deputy. "Linus, get Miss Danaher a chair so she can sit down."

The deputy placed his papers on the sheriff's desk and brought a chair from the corner. He set it down facing the desk. I thanked the deputy.

"Would you care for some coffee?" the sheriff asked indicating the pot on the stove nearby. "Made it less than an hour ago. Still fresh."

I told him I did not care for any.

The sheriff glanced over at his deputy and said, "The blankets in the cells need airing out."

"Right now?" the deputy asked.

Sheriff Martínez scowled at the deputy who sniffed, took a ring of keys from the wall, and unlocked the heavy door. I saw the door was covered with iron plating. A number of dents and scratches were in evidence on it, as though would-be prisoners had kicked in protest at being hauled away. The deputy pulled the door open, and a stale smell invaded the room as he went out. The door shut with a hollow metal clang.

Sheriff Martínez took a breath and said, "Police Chief Chavez and myself are working very hard to catch the man responsible."

"I'm glad to know that."

"I won't lie to you, Miss Danaher. Time has not been kind to us. It's been over a month since your sister was attacked. We think robbery is one possibility. Another is that the man tried to force himself on Mrs. Preston. In either case we believe she probably fought back."

I nodded my understanding and clasped my hands together in my lap.

"We've asked around the district over there by the river, three or four times, did you see anyone that night? Anything suspicious?" He shook his head. "Nobody saw anything. Some said they thought they heard coyotes. Or they were asleep. One old man claimed he saw a *fantasma*."

"Pardon me?"

"Oh, a phantom. A ghost. This man, he likes his liquor and, well, he's claimed to see a lot of things."

"I see," I said, disappointed. I no more believed in ghosts than the banshee or the death coach. Ghosts exist in one of Mother's favorite stories, Mr. Charles Dickens's *A Christmas Carol*. And a fine job they do showing Mr. Scrooge the error of his greedy ways. But there are no ghosts. Not real ones.

"Chief Chavez and two of his men were already at Mr. Preston's home when I got there. We went down to the river with torches to look for tracks, but it started raining very hard. That thunderstorm washed away any sign we might have followed. We found no evidence of vagrants or much else."

I saw his jaw tighten.

He went on. "It does not appear that anything was stolen from your sister so we have nothing to look for, nothing someone might try to sell or trade. Nothing at all, I'm afraid."

He rubbed his finger across his mouth. I thought he was considering something more to tell me, but he dropped his hand down to his desk and I concluded this interview was over with. I stood up to leave.

"Your sister didn't have any enemies that we could find," he said.

"Thank you. I appreciate that, sheriff."

"But her husband, he does."

"Well, attorneys can lose cases. I understand that."

"It's not that Mr. Preston lost cases, it's that he won them."

I settled back into the chair.

"There are a lot of people here that don't like your brother-in-law," he said, "and there are many others who are scared of him.

"Scared? Of Charles?"

"That's right."

"But why?"

"He wields a lot of power around here. Him. Mr. Catron."

"I still don't understand."

"Have you heard of the Santa Fe Ring?"

"No," I said.

"Some people have lost their homes, their land, all their money in court cases these men have handled. And this Santa Fe Ring—Mr. Catron, your brother-in-law and a few others—they've made considerable money from those cases. Land grants, a good portion of them."

"What are land grants?"

He did his best to explain, and I did my best to follow. These grants were composed of sprawling tracts of land given to favored people over the years, first by the Spanish kings and later by the Mexican government. Some were hundreds of acres, and others covered thousands of acres.

"When the Americans took over this territory, the problems started," he said.

These land grants he mentioned had strange sounding names. Anton Chico. Tierra Amarilla. Petaca. Many others. He talked about taxes and surveys and deeds. The Spanish grants and Mexican deeds were not so sophisticated as those drawn up by the Americans, he said. The papers they were written on showed landmarks designating the boundaries. A mountain, a stand of trees, the bend of a stream.

"For years," he said, "these landmarks were never questioned, but when the Americans arrived, men like Catron and your brother-in-law said these landmarks were unacceptable. New surveys were needed. Catron has friends in Congress in Washington, and he got them involved. That's when the court cases started. New surveys were conducted. Fees and taxes needed to be paid. That's when things started getting complicated."

It all sounded so confusing. "Sheriff, might I trouble you for some water?" I asked.

He filled a cup for me and poured himself some coffee.

"You see," he said, "some of the landowners paid with cash money and others offered land as payment to Catron and your brother-in-law and these other Ring men. They accepted hundreds of acres. Cases dragged on and some got settled, usually with the land grant owners and their families losing." He shook his head. "They had to sell their land for pennies. You can guess who bought it up. Catron and Preston became two of the biggest landowners in the territory. Hundreds of thousands of acres. Those two have made more money than I could ever hope to see. A lot of people lost their land and homes. Some of them believe they were cheated." He took a sip of his coffee. "A bad situation. *Muy mal.* Very bad. People can turn desperate, Miss Danaher."

Good Lord above. Had Charles purposely swindled people? Was that how he had come by all his money and house and property?

The sheriff took several sheets of paper from his desk drawer. "We had a man come in who swore he saw your brother-in-law by the river the night of your sister's attack."

"What?"

"It's what I'm trying to tell you. It's right here," he said, looking over the papers. "The man making the claim lost his case in court to Preston a couple of months ago. He made no secret of the fact he would make him pay. And we know Preston was nowhere near the river that night."

"He told me he left for Denver earlier that day," I said.

"That's right. We have statements from the clerk at the depot here in town who saw him board the train, and there's the conductor who was on the train Preston took to Denver. Both are reputable men." He slid the papers back into the drawer. "Do you want to hear the rest?"

"You mean there's more?"

A disquieting look shadowed his face.

I looked at my hands in my lap and wagged my head. Charles. This place. It was all more baffling than ever. Had I not known better, I might truly believe God had abandoned this blighted place.

"Please, go on," I said.

"There are those who claim this Ring has ordered men killed."

Words failed me. I stared at him in disbelief.

The sheriff continued. "They say the Ring had Billy the Kid killed over in Lincoln County a couple of years ago. And before that up in Colfax County, a Mexican named Manuel Cardenas was gunned down while in the custody of the sheriff there. There's others said to be on a list."

"But, but why would they do such a thing?"

"These Ring men run things around here. They don't want to see that disturbed. The Kid had been stirring up trouble for them for a long time. And I know for a fact a lot of people in this territory thought highly of the Kid, and bitter feelings have not abated over his killing. As I told you, this Ring wields a lot of power, and that scares folks."

"But you said yourself there's no proof of any of it. Somebody says this, others believe that, and this one claims something else."

"That's true, but there's no denying that people have lost their homes and men are dead. No contesting either of those. And people are angry. Mostly people who had too much to drink or just wanting to vent their anger have made threats. But sometimes it can be more serious." He drew his lips tight. "As much as I hate to say this, Miss Danaher, it might be that someone went after your sister to get back at your brother-in-law."

I thought I must have misunderstood him. Had he said what I thought he said? The sheriff kept speaking but his voice was just a dull distant rumbling to me. Everything, all of it seemed too fantastic, too inconceivable. Brigid killed because of actions Charles might have taken? How could it be?

It was a few moments before the sheriff's words became clear to me again. I also realized the deputy had returned and was leaning against the desk across the way.

"Been a black mark on our city," Sheriff Martínez was saying. "We will find the man who did this."

The deputy spoke up. "And when we find him, we'll give him a fair trial and then we'll give him a good hanging."

I looked back at him.

He gave me a toothy grin. "My pappy used to say you give folks what they want, and they'll show up."

From behind the steel door came that sound like a rooster crowing again. And then a different sound, like a dog barking.

"Linus," the sheriff said, "go back there and shut that son of—" He glanced at me. "That *loco* peanut vendor up."

Snatching the key ring, the deputy left the room, muttering under his breath.

"We will catch this fiend who killed your sister, I promise you," the sheriff said.

"Do you think my sister's children are in any danger?" I asked.

"Truthfully, no. I wouldn't worry too much."

The sound of the barking continued, and I heard the deputy shout something. Abrupt silence followed.

# *Chapter Nineteen*

Outside the sheriff's office, Mr. Jessup assisted me into the surrey. My face must have looked troubled for he asked me if everything was all right. I told him what the sheriff had said to me, about these land grants and some people losing all they had. "He said someone might have killed my sister because of something Charles had done to them. He also said that people are afraid of Mr. Catron and Charles."

Mr. Jessup pushed his big *sombrero* back on his head and narrowed his eyes at me. "Do you recall me telling you about that house Mr. Preston bought?"

"The one on Johnson Street."

"That's the one. I told you he got it from Mr. Catron who got it through a court settlement deal."

I nodded.

"The man who owned that house later claimed Mr. Catron stole it out from under him. The man said Mr. Catron and the judge were in cahoots and cheated him out of his place."

"Was it true?" I asked.

"It depends on who you talk to. You see, there's those that say the lawyers and judges and politicians around here run everything."

"Yes, the sheriff said this Ring has a lot of power in this town."

"To hear some tell it, it's more like the whole Territory."

"Did you say the Territory?"

"Yes, ma'am. Every acre."

"I don't—How—?"

"Like I said ma'am, some are certain these lawyers and politicians got their hands in almost every business. Courts, cattle, goods, land."

"And Charles is part of this Ring, this corruption?"

"There are all kinds of rumors."

"Well, is there any truth to these rumors?"

"That's the rub of it. To my mind, there's always somebody running things, somebody in charge. And there's always somebody else feeling they got the short end of a deal. You ask me, it's just the way things are. Long as there's people, that's how it's going to be."

"So, you're saying he is involved."

"I'm saying rumors abide in this Territory."

"Like rumors about this Ring having people killed?"

"Our sheriff. He's a bleak one, isn't he? Did he mention that he's a Democrat and Mr. Preston and Mr. Catron are Republicans?

I shook my head.

"Well, there's strong antagonism between those two parties around here. I've heard each side call the other everything from the lowest form of snake in creation to half-breed sons of prostitutes. Does this Ring exist?" He shrugged. "I got no proof either way. But people will believe what they want to believe, same as a rumor. Of course, that's only my opinion."

I did not know what to make of all this talk about murder and swindles. A lot of conjecture and suspicion is what it sounded like. This land business and court cases could have been bad luck as much as anything. Coincidence might have just as easily played a part, as well. And saying a murder was ordered was a far cry from proving it.

"Where to next, ma'am?"

I said I wanted to speak with the doctor who treated my sister after her attack.

"That would be Doc Symington," he said. He mentioned something about this being Wednesday and the doctor being at his home instead of at St. Vincent's Hospital. My mind was elsewhere, though.

Did Brigid know how Charles made his money? About this Ring of charlatans and swindlers? No, wait. That was unfair. There was no proof of this Ring. But certainly, she would have asked him, wouldn't she? Mr. Jessup said this whole country is filled with rumors. But surely, she had been aware of them. How could she not? She would have asked Charles if this Ring did indeed exist and was he a party to it. She would ask him about those things she had heard. Was there any truth to them? And what about the money to build this mansion? It had to come from somewhere. Brigid was no fool. She would have asked him about it, as well. And what would Charles have answered?

Good Lord, who was I kidding? Charles would avoid and evade, just as he had done with me. Tell only what he needed to say and nothing more. And if Brigid persisted so much as a syllable, Charles would probably have—No, I refused to speculate about that. It was not my place to imagine discussions between my sister and her husband. Especially since I had a low opinion of Charles. But I knew my questions would only persist and fester. Brigid simply had to have asked Charles. Perhaps the children had heard—

"Ma'am?"

"I'm sorry, Mr. Jessup. What was that?"

"I thought I heard you asking about the children."

"No, I—no." My Lord, had I been thinking out loud?

We were passing a row of shabby dwellings, all under one long flat roof. I saw a couple of people wrapped in blankets asleep in chairs or sitting propped up by their doorways. Chickens scratched at barren ground.

I believe Mr. Jessup told me Doctor Symington lived near the *plaza*. Was it on Grant Street? Lincoln Avenue? I couldn't recall, but the towers of the cathedral loomed up in the distance off to my right.

A minute later we pulled in front of Doctor Symington's home with its cracked *adobe* brick walls. The sad-looking exterior of the house was relieved by the splashes of color amid the flowerbeds in front of the weathered wooden porch. Half of the blooms had already fallen off, but it was still a pleasure to see, a relief even, in light of my conversation with the sheriff. A woman came out the front door. She wore a work dress and a wide straw hat. In each hand she carried a watering pot.

"Good afternoon, Mrs. Symington!" Mr. Jessup called out as we climbed down from the surrey.

She smiled. "Ah, *Señor* Jessup," she said and set the pots down.

Mrs. Symington was a handsome Mexican woman with a delightful sparkle in her eyes. "And who have you brought with you?" she asked.

We reached the front porch and Mr. Jessup made the introductions and the reason for the visit. Mrs. Symington expressed her sympathies and invited Mr. Jessup and I inside. He said he wanted to water the horses and would be along.

Going inside, Mrs. Symington asked me to wait while she went to get her husband. I admit I was truly surprised at what I saw for this was not the mud house I expected. A beautiful fountain gurgled in a small courtyard beyond the entryway. The home surrounded the open courtyard with its stone walkway and potted flowers. What a grand idea.

Doctor Symington appeared from a side room. He took the cigar from his mouth. He had kind eyes and pronounced ears.

"My wife told me why you've come," Doctor Symington said cordially and led me into his office.

A large desk faced the door. There were also two chairs, an examination table, and a glass-faced cabinet with various colored bottles on the shelves. A box of toys sat off to the side of his desk. I spied a doll and some wooden soldiers. They must be for the children who came to see him. On the wall by his desk was his framed diploma. By the window hung a cross. The heady smell of tobacco lingered in the air. He stubbed out the cigar and opened the window. It helped some. We sat down.

"How much would you like me to tell you," he asked.

"Everything," I replied. "Every detail."

His shirtsleeves were rolled up and he liked to motion with his hands while he spoke.

"Your sister's injuries indicated she had fought with someone. Whoever it was had tried to drown her as she had water in her lungs. White foam had bubbled up out of her mouth when I first saw her. There were also scratches and abrasions on her arms and neck. Some of them deep. She was struck with a rock, here." Using his fingers, he indicated the left side of his head. "The blow to her head is what eventually killed her. It was a heavy blow and fractured her skull. I managed to stop the bleeding, but the swelling persisted. I don't know how she held on as long as she did to tell you the honest truth."

I asked the doctor if it was possible Brigid was purposely hit with a rock or if she fell and struck her head.

"Hard to say. When they find the swine who did it, we'll get the answers."

Mrs. Symington appeared in the doorway carrying a tray with a plate of cookies and a pot of tea and cups and saucers.

"She made the cookies herself," he said.

"They are called *biscochitos*," she said as she left the room. "My Mother taught me how to make them."

I was not very hungry or thirsty, but I did not wish to be rude. Those cookies were indeed crisp and tasty, and the tea soothing.

"Brigid spoke of you often," Doctor Symington said after a short silence. "She said you were the steady one."

I felt my soul ache. My hand rose to my chest. Tears welled. So many thoughts rushed to my mind. Oh, dear Brigid, how I wished you were still here.

The doctor continued. "She told me she wouldn't be surprised if you were running the Sisters of Mercy one day."

"Did you know my sister well?" I asked, trying to keep the words from catching in my throat.

He smiled at me. "I brought both Matthew and Anne into this world. She loved them so. The joy of her life."

"What about Charles?"

He covered his mouth with his hand and looked down at the top of his desk, as though searching for the words.

"Nice looking fellow," he finally said. "Successful law practice. Likes things his way. I... well, I should leave it at that."

"Please, Doctor. What is it?"

He blew out a long breath. "I shouldn't tell you this, but I thought very highly of your sister, and I did my best to protect her."

"Protect her? From what?"

"From Charles. He came to see me more than a few times. For some treatments."

"What kind of treatments?"

"He started frequenting a couple of places down on Palace. Palace Avenue, I mean. They are, well, I don't mean to give offense, but what we call a—"

"Brothel?"

Doctor Symington's face registered surprise.

"We have them in Pittsburgh, too," I said. "The Sisters of Mercy dispense comfort and care to all, regardless of condition. Please, Doctor, don't tell me he gave something to my sister."

He nodded. "Syphilis. I was treating her, too."

My heart felt like it had been stabbed with a knife.

Doctor Symington said he started her treatments back in December. "They were hard on her. She took to her bed for weeks."

December. Last winter then. That explained why Brigid wrote to me saying she could not come to see Mother when she had taken ill with pneumonia, and why Brigid could not attend Mother's funeral. Damn you, Charles, for the shame and hurt you brought to my sister.

"Later your sister told me there was no more love between her and Charles," Doctor Symington said. "Matthew and Anne were all she had left. And then it was around April, I think, Charles started going out of town every couple of months for a week or more to Denver. He said it was business, but there's been talk."

"You mean talk he's seeing another woman?"

"I'm sorry to say that it is."

"Did my sister know?"

He looked at me. I saw the answer in his eyes.

That talk of another woman was just gossip, but I could only imagine the pain it caused my sister. However, all the rest of what Doctor Symington had told me was no rumor. There were no whispered suspicions or speculations to consider. The kind doctor's words confirmed to me that Charles was among the lowest of the low. A rogue. A cur. The contemptible bastard. Even as the words came to me, none of them contained the considerable malice and seething anger I felt toward Charles. Mother Superior always told us to love the sinner but hate the sin, but I could find no Christian charity in my heart for him. If he were standing in front of me at this very moment, I would have slapped his despicable face. Twice.

I thanked the Doctor and his wife for their hospitality.

Mr. Jessup waited at the surrey. I looked him straight in the eye and asked him to please tell me the truth, did he know about Charles's activities at the Palace Avenue brothels.

He neither flinched nor backed away. "Yes," he said. "Mrs. Medrano and me both knew. Understand, it doesn't mean we liked it, but there was nothing we could do. I can't say I'm proud of not saying something but, well, we work for Mr. Preston. We like our jobs. And the children. And we liked Mrs. Preston."

I believed his words were honest.

"And I'll tell you this, too, ma'am," he said. "For all Mr. Preston has, I say your sister deserved better."

I appreciated his kind words and told him so. But God help me, I did not know what I would do about Charles when he returned from his "business dealings" in Denver.

# Chapter Twenty

"**S**piegelberg Brothers store is just over there, ma'am," Mr. Jessup said, pointing to it across the *plaza*. "You said you needed some new dresses."

"No, not now," I said. It was already half past two o'clock. Mr. Jessup would have to go get the children soon. Besides, there would be time to think about myself later.

A sudden wind swept across the *plaza*, nearly whisking my hat off my head. I put my hand on top of my hat to hold it in place. The wind grew worse. Those on the *plaza* made for the cover of doorways. One man chased a newspaper that had gotten away from him, retrieving the pages when they plastered themselves against the white picket fence surrounding the *plaza*.

"This wind is terrible," I said, getting a mouthful of dust as I did so.

"It blows like the devil here, ma'am." Mr. Jessup hurried the horses along.

Leaves swirled and blew across the grounds of St. Vincent's Hospital. A sister pushed an old man in a wheelchair to the main doors. She ducked her head against the wind and a gust caught the long black cape she wore and whipped it around, enveloping the poor man in the chair.

Leaving me at the house, Mr. Jessup went to get Matthew and Anne at their schools. Inside, I found Mrs. Medrano in the large parlor, the burgundy one that had been intended to host dances. She was rolling up the rugs in preparation for sweeping the floor. Outside the windows the tree branches shook as the wind buffeted the house.

"You were gone a long time. I hope everything went well," she said.

I told her I was very touched that the children had the angels carved on Brigid's headstone.

"*Sí.* They thought their mother would like them."

I nodded. "I also know about Charles and my sister."

A look of apprehension crossed her face.

"The treatments," I said. "I spoke with Doctor Symington."

Her small shoulders slumped, and she cast her eyes down. "I am so sorry, Miss Danaher. I wanted to tell you but —"

"Please," I said cutting her off. "I understand. Mr. Jessup told me everything."

She took a handkerchief from the end of her sleeve and wiped her eyes. "*Los niños.*" She made a frustrated gesture. "Oh, my Spanish again. I am trying to say it is the children we stay for more than anything."

"I'm certain Brigid knows that, too, and she's very grateful, as am I."

Turning, I saw the portrait of Brigid over the great marble fireplace. I stepped closer. Those eyes of hers were so full of sadness.

"When did you tell me this was painted?" I asked.

"Almost a year ago."

A year ago. I recalled Mrs. Medrano had also said that Brigid had not wanted her portrait painted. Doctor Symington had told me he began treating Brigid last winter. Had she sat for this portrait about the time she first knew of Charles's unfaithfulness? Perhaps the answer was there, in the portrait, staring directly at me, as to the reason for the dark melancholy in her eyes.

# Chapter Twenty-One

As quickly as that wind had come up it had died down considerably. It wasn't long before Mr. Jessup returned with the children. I was in the tower sitting room. Matthew was the first through the door. He appeared disheveled with his shirt and trousers dirty and smudged. I asked him what happened.

"Nothing," he said and ran upstairs.

Anne stood in the hallway, her face long and sad, her eyes following her brother up the stairs. His door slammed shut and Anne looked at me. I asked her if she knew why her brother was so upset. She said that she had heard that some of the boys at his school were picking on him. "It's been going on a long time. That's what one of my friends told me."

"But why are they picking on him?" I asked as Mr. Jessup came in through the front door carrying a basket filled with firewood.

Anne shook her head.

I told her to go on upstairs.

"Pardon me, ma'am," Mr. Jessup said, "is it all right if I go up and put more firewood in your room for this evening?"

"It's not necessary. I didn't light a fire last night."

He stood there, like something was on his mind.

"Mr. Jessup?"

"It may not be my place," he said, "but it's about Matthew."

"Anne said he was being picked on at school. Do you know something about it?"

He said sometimes boys pick out someone to see what they can get away with, or to see what another boy is made of. "Matthew's a slight lad. That doesn't make it any easier for him."

I asked if Charles hadn't had a talk with Matthew, to explain such things.

Mr. Jessup said he had heard Charles tell his son it was against the rules of the school to fight. "He also told him any sort of brawling would bring shame and embarrassment on him, meaning Mr. Preston, and he would not allow that."

I held my tongue as to what I thought Charles should or should not allow, let alone be embarrassed about.

"Did my sister know about of any of this?"

"I believe she did, but she was in such bad shape."

"She knew and she tried to help Matthew." It was Mrs. Medrano. I turned to face her.

"She told Matthew not to take anything from the other boys, to stand up to the bullies," she said.

"Then why doesn't he?"

She let a heavy sigh. "He wants the love of a father who won't give it to him. Or to Anne, either."

I glanced at Mr. Jessup who nodded sadly in agreement.

\*   \*   \*

At supper that night, Mrs. Medrano set bowls of beef stew before the children and I as we sat down at the dining room table. She told me she had left the peppers out of my stew. I thanked her for her thoughtfulness.

135

I said grace, noting that Matthew kept his eyes fixed on some spot on the tabletop.

Mrs. Medrano brought out a round loaf of bread that had failed to rise much, though she seemed quite pleased with the results. Cutting several slices, she encouraged me to take one. Lifting it from the plate I was unprepared for the grayish-blue color of the bread.

"Try some honey with it," Mrs. Medrano said, passing me the dish of honey and a spoon.

"I've never seen bread like this," I said.

"I make it with blue corn meal."

With some trepidation I spooned a bit of honey onto the bread and took a bite. It had a delightful flavor and I told her so.

Anne accepted a slice of the bread but made several worried glances at her brother who was pushing the stew in his bowl around with his fork, his agitation apparent.

"Mrs. Medrano," I said, "this is delicious. We have nothing like it in Pittsburgh."

She smiled but cast concerned looks, first at the children and then at me.

Perhaps my coaxing worked, for Matthew took a bite of stew. I offered him the blue bread, but he shook his head. At least he was eating something.

Anne appeared less tense now and asked for some of honey for her bread. As I passed her the dish, Matthew bolted from the room.

"Matthew!" Mrs. Medrano said.

"No," I said. "Let him be."

He stomped up the staircase. The sound of his bedroom door slamming shut made Anne jump and she shut her eyes tight.

"You don't have to stay if you don't wish to," I told her.

She scooted off her chair and left the table, wiping her eyes. At the entryway, she stopped and said, "I'm sorry I'm not very hungry."

The poor dears, I thought. They are so lost.

# Chapter Twenty-Two

Soon enough it was time for the children to do their school lessons. I took them into the green sitting room and lit the kindling in the fireplace as the evening had turned chilly. We spent a quiet half hour there, the room warming nicely. I made no comment about Matthew's eyes being red, likely from crying up in his room after supper. Anne noticed them and looked at me, the question plain on her face asking what was wrong with her brother. I made a gesture that she not worry. To bring it up in front of her would have only embarrassed Matthew, making him feel worse than I suspected he already did.

After completing their lessons, I sent them off to wash their faces and get ready for bed.

Shortly, I went up to see to the children. Entering Anne's room, I heard her saying her prayers, asking God to bless Father, Matthew, Mrs. Medrano, Mr. Jessup and Aunt Catherine. "And please," she said, "tell mama I miss her."

A fine daughter you raised, Brigid.

Anne climbed into bed, pulled up the covers and asked me if Matthew was all right. I told her he was just sad and that boys deal with their sadness differently than girls. The look on her face said she accepted my explanation. Then a worried frown appeared. She said, "Where's Casie?"

"Who is Casie?"

"My dolly."

Of course, the dolly with the golden hair she held close the night before. I looked about and saw it on the shelf near the fireplace where a comforting fire burned. Handing her the dolly I said, "Casie is a fine Irish name. Do you know the meaning of it?"

She shook her head.

"It means brave."

A big smile spread across Anne's face.

I said, "Do you know what your name means?"

"Mama told me it means joy."

"That it does. It was your grandmother's name. Did you know that?"

She nodded. "Mama told me I was named after her. I wish I could have met her."

"I'm certain she does, too, sweetheart." I ran my fingers over her cheek. "You know your mother's name was Brigid. That means strength and virtue.

"I like that," she said. "What does Matthew mean?"

"Matthew was one of the twelve apostles. His name means gift of God."

"What about your name?"

My name meant pure, but I did not wish to put a notion into her head that I was some sort of saint. I said, "Catherine means I have to try very hard to be a good person."

I expected she was about to ask about her Father's name. Mother had made me look into the name of Charles when he was prowling around Brigid. I dreaded having to tell my niece it meant man, though Charles was no sort of decent man, at least in my estimation. Instead, she asked, "Did you and my mama have dolls?"

"That we did."

"What were their names?"

"Your Mother's doll's name was Nell. It means champion. I named my doll Mavie."

"What does that mean?"

"Songbird."

"Can you sing?"

"Not a note."

Anne giggled as sweetly as I had ever heard.

"Aunt Catherine, can you tell me a bedtime story?"

I told her I knew many of them and asked her if she thought her brother would like to hear one, as well. Anne said that he used to, but when he turned nine, he decided he was too old for such things. I hid my disappointment at that.

"Well, what kind of stories did your Mother tell you?" I wondered if Brigid had introduced her children to Father's tales of howling banshees and vengeful ghosts.

"Stories about good witches and kind leprechauns. Irish stories," Anne said.

Clearly Brigid had made some changes to Father's tales. Witches were terrible creatures, hags that smelled of the grave. They cast many a malignant spell using a hand cut from a corpse. And a kind leprechaun, was it? No such thing existed. A stumpy, slouching, mischief-making trickster was how Father described them. Yet, a leprechaun cobbles as fine a pair of shoes as you could ever wear. He grows rich from the chore and hoards his gold in a treasure-crock he keeps buried in a secret place. Only the threat of a slow death roasting on the gridiron will make him reveal his hidden trove.

Looking down at Anne's glowing little face anticipating a warmhearted Irish tale to send her off to sleep, I knew I must think quickly. A fable of Aesop's might have to do. But an idea came to me. I remembered a story my fellow sisters and I had seen in the Pittsburgh newspaper some months past. It told of a small township east of the city where a horrible man tried to exact a toll to cross a public bridge and claimed later it was only a practical joke. Yes, a story of the far darrig would do nicely, it being an ill-natured and foul little jokester, a cousin to the leprechaun.

I sat on the edge of Anne's bed and began. "Near the emerald mountain of Ben Bulben in County Sligo, the village of Drumcliff sat perched upon a low ridge. Flowing past the village was a river so grand it was given the name Codnach, which everyone knew meant princely river. The salmon and trout inhabiting the river were much prized throughout Ireland for they were both the largest and the tastiest fish in the land."

Anne nestled down under the covers, her eyes fixed upon me.

"At a bend of the river stood a stone bridge," I went on. "This spot was considered the best place to catch the fish. The best catcher of these fish was a young girl by the name of Grace. Known throughout the county she was.

"One morning, with her pole in hand, Grace went to the bridge and was surprised to find a gate barring her way."

"How did the gate get there?" Anne asked.

"Have patience. I'm getting to it," I said and continued the tale. "Not seeing anyone about and not one to remain flustered for long, Grace crawled under the gate and started over the bridge to take her favorite spot. Tossing her line into the water, she was startled by a booming voice coming from underneath the bridge demanding, 'Who dares to cross my bridge without paying the toll?'

"'Who is that?' Grace called out.

"'It is I,' came the answer. 'Bram Balor!'

"Grace looked down and saw Bram Balor scurry out from under

141

the bridge, brandishing a gnarled shillelagh at her. Bram Balor was a far darrig, a rat boy, named as such for he was a motley creature with hairy skin and a long snout, and he wore a red hat and—" I stopped. Anne's eyes had grown wide. I asked her if something was the matter.

With a quivering voice she said, "Is it a monster?"

"The far darrig?"

She responded with the slightest of nods.

"There are those who might call it a kind of monster, I suppose."

"I don't like monsters."

"You don't like monsters, is it?" I said gently.

She shook her head.

This was a fine predicament. "Would it make you feel better if I told you now that the monster is vanquished?"

She nodded her head vigorously, but I could still see she was frightened.

"Perhaps we shall leave it at that then."

"What happens to Grace?" she asked, sitting up in the bed. "The monster doesn't get her, does it?"

"Oh, no. Grace is the heroine of the tale. She saves her family from the clutches of the beast."

"Good. I'm glad," she said and laid herself back down.

I could see something was on her mind from the way she drew her lips tight.

"Are you going to go away?" she asked.

I cannot deny the question startled me. "Of course not. What gave you the idea I would do such a thing?"

"Mama went away."

There it was. The thing every child dreads. Sometimes my orphan girls would ask me that very same question. I gave her the answer I gave to each of them. "Sweetheart, I will always be here for you, no matter what."

A sharp pang of guilt struck my heart, for I had left my girls behind at St. Paul's without so much as a word of good-bye. Hurt was hurt, regardless of the reasons. God please, give me strength.

I tucked Anne in. Reaching the door to leave, I heard Anne say in a sleepy whisper, "Thank you for the story, Aunt Catherine. I liked most of it."

# Chapter Twenty-Three

The hurried sound of paper rustling and the abrupt extinguishing of candlelight greeted me as I opened the door to Matthew's room. The fire in the fireplace cast a steady glow and I caught the sudden stillness of movement in his bed. I had seen this before at night with some of my orphan girls, that moment when they try to pretend to be asleep, knowing full well they have been caught doing something they shouldn't.

Stepping closer, I could not help but notice the wispy trail of smoke gently wafting up from the candle on the table by his bedside. Matthew appeared to be asleep, but I knew he was not. I decided maybe it was best to let him be. Turning away, I caught sight of something sticking out from underneath his pillow. I craned my head around. It looked familiar. The shadow looming, a frightened face, the words "Constance Wiley" and "black mesa." Mr. Fairchild's book.

"I met the author, you know," I said softly. "Fletcher Fairchild."

A moment passed. Matthew rolled over, a frown on his face. "You really did?"

"On the train ride here. The cover of his book looks very frightening, don't you think?"

He sat up and pulled it from under his pillow. Holding it in his hands, he kept his eyes down.

"How is it?" I asked.

"I like it. It's exciting." His head jerked up. "You aren't going to tell Father, are you?"

"And why would I do that?"

"He doesn't approve of these stories."

"Did he give you a reason?"

"I was sent home from school last month for having one in my bag. The Christian Brothers say they pollute the mind. Father agrees."

"Well, let's take a look then, shall we, and see?"

Matthew hesitated, unsure of my intentions, I suspected, and then handed it to me.

Opening it, I found the corner of a page folded down. I began reading from the page out loud, but quietly so as not to disturb Anne in her room.

"The sound of a snapping twig close by shrouded Constance with fear. In the early moonlight, she saw the shade coming toward her. Nearer it approached and she stepped away until she felt the cold stone of the boulder against her back barring any further retreat.

"The shade drew closer, and she was enabled to recognize the Indian, his face in full war paint. It was Red Tomahawk, the Comanche, looking like the devil himself. Blood smeared his buckskin tunic. Reeking scalps dangled from his beaded belt.

"A shiver of dread coursed through Constance. What horror would the savage do? What advantage would he take of her helplessness? She saw the silvery glint of a knife in his hand.

"Constance refused to die without a word of protest and thrusting her head back defiantly declared, 'Harm me and you will pay dearly!'

"His eyes filled with hate, the painted Comanche let out a fierce howl and raised his knife to plunge the flashing blade into her heart when the ground trembled with the thunder of hoof beats and Ranger Dan Joyner appeared astride his white steed, a six-shooter in his hand and a cry on his lips, 'Curse you Red Tomahawk! Let that woman go!'

"'You will die, paleface!' Red Tomahawk shouted and leapt at the young Texas Ranger.

"The scene that followed was too horrible to describe, but suffice to say Constance was rescued by Dan Joyner, yet only to find themselves facing the evil and vicious..."

I could not bear to turn the page. Mr. Fairchild's writing was as lurid as the cover of his book.

"Do you like these stories?" I asked.

"There's lots of excitement and danger," Matthew said. "The hero gets into bad scrapes but always manages to save everyone."

"That's a good thing, isn't it?"

He nodded. "It's how it should be."

I handed the book back to him. "I think so, too. You keep this book but leave it here. Don't take it to school."

His face registered surprise. "But what about Father?"

"It'll be our secret."

# Chapter Twenty-Four

Shortly thereafter in my room, I opened the Divine Office and knelt beside my bed and said my nightly prayer. Closing the book, I set it aside and clasped my hands together for a different prayer.

"Dear Lord," I began, "You've sent me here to help Matthew and Anne, to protect them, to shield them, to comfort them as their Mother would have done. I humbly ask that You guide me in that endeavor and to make this a happy family again. God bless Matthew, Anne, Mrs. Medrano, and Mr. Jessup. And God bless Mother Superior, Sister Agatha, and little Eleanor and Martha and all the others at St. Paul's.

"And now, Lord, a word about Charles. I know that harboring ill will is not a Christian act, and I am keenly aware that my stubborn ways are set as right as stone, so I ask You, please, show me the way to forgive his sinfulness and to stop hoping he burns in hell for all eternity. In the name of the Father, and of the Son, and of the Holy Ghost. Amen."

Blowing out the candle I slipped under the bedcovers. A chill permeated the room and I thought of lighting the fire in the fireplace but decided my covers would do just as well to keep me warm and soon sleep overtook me.

\* \* \*

I bolted upright. The house shook as though a cannon ball had struck it and the wind churned anew, like Satan himself was creating a gale storm. A terrible row it was. Pittsburgh received its share of wind when storms approached, but even those winds were nothing compared to this.

A vigorous tapping drew my attention to my door. I threw off the covers and crossed the room. Opening the door, I saw little Anne in her nightdress and the fear on her face.

"What's the matter, sweetheart?" I asked.

"Can I sleep with you, please?"

"Did the wind scare you?"

"There's something outside my window."

"It was probably just something blown by."

She shook her head. "I saw a face. Looking at me."

A face? Had someone climbed up the wall outside? No, of course not, but I thought I better go have a look, so Anne would know it was safe.

"You wait here," I said, and she ran over, climbed into my bed and pulled up the covers.

I struck a match and lit the candle. Stepping into the hallway, I went to her open door and peered into her bedroom. Except for the wind all was still. The window curtains were wide open. I raised the candle and approached the window. The wind rose, and outside tree branches shook. I saw no figure scurrying about, nothing out of the ordinary. Beyond the road stood the wall of the archbishop's garden. No strange person or movement there, either.

Returning to my room I found Anne sitting pensively on my bed. I told her I looked all around. "There is nothing there to worry about.

It's only the—"

Anne gasped. Something was behind me. A presence. I spun around and saw Matthew standing the doorway, trying hard not to appear frightened.

"What is it, Matthew?"

"Someone is outside. I heard them."

"I told you someone is out there," Anne cried.

"Now the two of you calm down," I said and asked Matthew to tell me exactly what he heard.

He said, "A voice. It was hard to hear but it sounded like it was saying, 'Children come play at the river.'"

Anne pulled the covers up over her mouth.

"They kept saying it," he went on, "I'm sorry, I got..." His chin began to tremble.

"No, you did right," I told him as I guided him to my bed. "I'm certain it's nothing. Just this wind."

I was trying to calm them and myself. Children come play at the river. Had Matthew truly heard such a thing? I could see he was plainly scared, as much as he tried to hide it. Leaving my door open as I went out, I told them to stay in my room and that everything would be fine.

In the hallway, candle in hand, I listened to see if Mrs. Medrano was moving about upstairs. Had all this awakened her? The wind stirred and howled outside, but I could catch no sound from the floor above me.

I stopped at the door of Matthew's bedroom. The covers of his bed were thrown back. The curtains half closed. A strong gust of wind buffeted the house and then quiet. I went to the window and listened. Not a sound. Pulling back the curtain, I saw only the moonlight reflected on the archbishop's garden wall and the road and grounds. I waited a few moments. Satisfied, I turned from the window and heard a cry that turned my blood cold. "Come play!" It sounded so clear.

Afraid I was to look out the window but forced myself to do so. I cast my eye about the grounds. I saw no one. No shadows moving about. Nothing. I held my breath. Straining to listen, my ear nearly touched the window. A shrieking blast of wind battered the glass, rattling it fiercely, as though someone were trying to break through it. I leapt back, nearly falling over Matthew's bed.

The wind blew hard again. It must have been the wind I heard. That was all. It had to be. There was no other explanation. This place played tricks. That I knew with certainty.

Back in my room, I assured the children they had no reason for concern.

"You didn't hear anything?" Matthew asked.

"Only the wind."

Mathew looked doubtful. Anne glanced from him to me. She was not convinced either.

"All right then," I said. "Would you like to sleep in here tonight?"

Anxious nods greeted me, and they scrambled under the covers.

I sat on the bed and placed the candle on the table. In spite of the vexing wind, I started to hum a lullaby I recalled Mother used to sing to Brigid and me when we couldn't sleep. As I mentioned before, I possessed no voice for singing, but I could hum on key. The tune was a sweet Irish one with a Gaelic name I could not recall.

"Mama sang that to us," Matthew said in a drowsy voice.

That made me smile. After a few minutes, the children were fast asleep.

I, however, was quite awake and decided to slip down to the kitchen and make myself a cup of tea in the hope it might help me to sleep.

With candle in hand, I descended the stairs and headed toward the dining room. I nearly cried out finding Mrs. Medrano seated at the table there enjoying a cup of tea and a slice of blue bread with honey.

"You cannot sleep, too?" she said.

Calming myself, I told her I could not. She offered to make me a cup of tea and said to help myself to the bread.

We sat at the table, and I told her about the children and their scare that night. When I finished, she said only that the wind does strange things.

I asked her if either Anne or Matthew had suffered from bad dreams over their Mother's attack or passing. I knew well enough there were times when a new girl would arrive at St. Paul's after the death of their only parent and the nightmares would come.

Mrs. Medrano hesitated. Did I see something behind her eyes?

"They both cried those first nights," she said. "And Matthew had trouble sleeping for a time."

"Did he say what was bothering him?"

"No. He has kept to himself."

"And Anne?"

"A few nights she came to me and said she was afraid of the dark."

"What did you do?"

"I sang to her until she fell back asleep."

"Have they said anything before about hearing things or seeing faces outside their windows?"

Mrs. Medrano shook her head. Getting to her feet, she went to a cabinet in the corner, opened it and took a bottle from a shelf.

"This might help you sleep," she said.

"What is it?"

"*Aguardente*. You call it brandy. It helps me when I cannot sleep. Would you like some in your tea?"

I knew brandy to be a stimulant, like alcohol and wine. We were to avoid all such beverages in the service of Christ. But I needed to sleep, and it was already past two in the morning.

"How much do you take?" I asked.

"Not much," she said.

"That sounds fine for me," I said and silently asked God for His understanding and forgiveness.

She poured about two spoonful's worth of the brandy into my cup and I took a tentative sip.

"Oh," I said, "that is good," and took another sip knowing full well Mother Superior would not approve.

"It was only the wind you heard," Mrs. Medrano said, putting the bottle back in the cabinet. "I am certain of it. It can be very bad."

# Chapter Twenty-Five

The sound of wood being sawed woke me the next morning. I slid carefully out from under the covers, as the children were still asleep in my bed. I kissed my Mother's crucifix, dressed and went downstairs, discovering the reason for the sawing, as well as the terrible noise that shook the house the night before. One of the tall cottonwood trees standing near Charles's study had been blown down during the windstorm. Long gnarled roots lay exposed from the torn-up ground. The tree had struck the side of the house, but caused little damage, at least that I could see.

Mr. Jessup directed the work of four men with long saws as they cut off the heavy branches.

"That wind was vicious last night," he said. "Took down a good tree."

When I asked how long it would take to remove it, he said they should have it cleared away by the afternoon.

The children appeared on the front porch. The sight of the stricken cottonwood saddened Anne while Matthew stared at it in wonder. Bustling them back inside, I told them to get themselves dressed and ready for school.

Up in my room I opened the Divine Office and prayed my morning prayer then washed my face and returned downstairs with the children.

Mrs. Medrano set plates of eggs and bacon and *tortillas* on the dining room table. We had breakfast and the mood of the children was considerably brighter.

After they left with Mr. Jessup for school, Mrs. Medrano asked me what magic I had done with them. "This is the first in a long time I have seen them happy."

"They were so frightened by the wind last night, I let them sleep in my bed."

Mrs. Medrano smiled knowingly. "Mrs. Preston would let them do that, too."

I was making headway with them then.

"There are still a few roses in bloom in the garden," she said. "After I clean the dishes, I will go pick some. They will look nice for the table."

I told her I would be glad to pick them as I had nothing to do until after Mr. Jessup returned. "He said he'd take me to town to get the new dresses."

Getting my sister's hat and taking a pair of shears and a basket from the back porch, I went into the garden and began my chore. While I could not see them, I did hear the workmen at the front of the house sawing up the tree.

The wind had scattered numerous rose petals about the grounds, more than I had thought when I first came outside, but I still found a number of roses unharmed. Placing them in my basket, I could not help feeling sad that my sister never had the opportunity to enjoy this garden. Her garden.

I spied several roses in a bed near the trellis. Going to it, I got down on my knees and carefully cut the stems, leaving them long for the tall vase Mrs. Medrano planned to put them in.

Performing this simple task, a tranquil feeling enveloped me.

Praying in the chapel at the convent back at St. Paul's was the only other time I experienced such serenity and joy. It was almost as though Brigid were present, and I was grateful for it.

Getting to my feet, I heard a strange sound, like a sharp thud against wood. Glancing about I saw nothing out of the ordinary when I heard it again. This time it was louder, and I caught movement. A grey stone rolled to a stop by the wooden bench under the trellis. Who threw it? And why? Down by the river something scurried behind a tree. I waited and watched. It was probably some rascal up to some mischief.

"Stop this foolishness and go home!" I called out.

Keeping a keen eye on the trees I expected to see the imp scamper off, but I saw no sign of him.

"I said go home now!" I called again.

Quiet was the response. I turned to go back to the house, and I heard it, clear as if the person was at my side whispering in my ear in a melodious voice. "He ohz."

Dropping my basket, I spun around. The air hung still. My breathing turned shallow. I could not hear the workmen. The world had gone silent.

"He ohz."

Rigid I stood, fighting down the fright trying take hold of me.

"This is not a joke!" I shouted.

A moment passed. The whisper came again, close by, only now the voice possessed a ragged coarseness. "He ohz!"

"Who's there?" I demanded.

A figure in black appeared from behind a tree. A black tattered veil covered the face, and a black garment, like a robe of some kind, torn and shredded, hung draped from the shoulders.

"Try may meese he ohz," came the coarse voice.

155

And through the black veil I could make out a face, a woman's face, but old and deeply creased, like some evil crone from a fairy tale. Was this real, or my imagination playing tricks again? The woman's mouth opened into a toothless grin. Good Lord! I had seen that face before. At the bridge near the train depot on the day I arrived. The old woman in the carriage that had nearly run us off the road! But how could this be? That woman had looked so frail and pitiful. The black figure disappeared behind a thick cottonwood.

I heard something different. Very faint.

"Mal dee tow."

What was it? Was that Spanish? What was happening here? Coarse laughter assaulted my ears.

"Stop this right now!" I shouted.

"Mal dee tow." That terrible whisper seemed to come from every direction, surrounding me.

I turned all about, searching for any movement, listening for telltale footfalls, the rustling of clothes. Nothing. Disquieting stillness enclosed me, as when I faced that raven here by the river, only now things had turned more ominous.

Hesitant, I took a step backward, keeping my eyes on the trees for movement and my ears alert for sound.

The black figure scurried past a cottonwood on the riverbank to my left. On my right a hissing noise startled me, then the sound of wood breaking somewhere in front of me.

"Mal dee tow."

"Stop it!" I shouted and felt my fright lessening and my ire rising. This game or whatever it was had gone on far too long. I heard the laughter, only now its coarseness held a jeering tone, mocking me. The figure showed itself, raised its black sleeve and beckoned, as though daring me to follow.

That was enough! Father and Mother did not raise their girls to be cowards.

I dropped the roses and gave chase. Laughing its cruel laugh, the black wretch weaved and dodged amid the cottonwood trees on the river's edge. Nimble and lithe, it seemed the wretch's feet barely touched the ground. I rounded a tree, and a low branch nearly took my hat off my head.

"I'll get you!" I shouted.

It neared the river then changed direction toward the dead misshapen tree. So close I was to it, I reached out my hand to take hold of its tattered robe when my foot caught on an exposed tree root. I fell forward with a groan. The black figure came from behind the tree and caught me by the arm. I struggled to pull free of its strong grasp and the black figure spoke.

"Careful, *mademoiselle*." The tone was strong yet friendly, and the accent decidedly French.

I stared at a row of crimson buttons and thin crimson piping against the blackness. Set back on the figure's head was not veil, but a wide brimmed black hat that kept the face in shadow. This was not the figure I had pursued, not the black shade that mocked and taunted me.

"Are you all right? What on earth were you chasing?" asked the figure.

"I'm fine," I said, steadying myself as the figure's hand released my arm. It was then I saw the gold ring of office on the fourth finger of the right hand and realized to my great embarrassment that this must be Archbishop Lamy. I knelt down to kiss the ring saying, "Forgive me, Your Excellency."

"No, no, please," he said and helped me to my feet.

His was a stern countenance with distinct cheekbones and a sharp chin. Flinty gray hair curled out from under his hat, but there was a kindness in his eyes.

"I was in my garden and heard a commotion," he said. "You're certain you are not injured?"

"No, Excellency, I'm not hurt."

Glancing about, searching the trees for that wretch in black, I said, "Please, did, did you see anyone here? Dressed in black?"

"Only myself, I'm afraid," he said.

"But surely you heard them."

"I believe it was only your shouts I heard. Whatever you were chasing is gone."

I apologized for disturbing him. But I could not help wondering how he had not heard what I had. Something was here, as God is my witness. I knew what I saw, black as night with a black veil covering the head, and then it disappeared, like a wisp of smoke in the wind.

"I know you know who I am," the archbishop said, "and if I were to make a guess, I'd say that you are Brigid's sister Catherine."

"I am," I said and felt my face flush at my lack of manners. "I'm sorry. I should have introduced myself right away."

He placed a gentle hand on mine and told me I was just as my sister had described me to him. "It has been my intention to come by and pay you a call," he went on. "But as you can tell I'm afraid I haven't been very successful. It's a pleasure to make your acquaintance."

"The pleasure is mine, Your Excellency."

"Here, I have something for you." He motioned for me to follow him. He moved with a quick and steady gait as we went around the wall of his garden to a doorway. The heavy-looking door lay open. Just inside the doorway he bent down for a few moments reaching into a basket I saw there. When he turned back, he held several bright red apples in his hands.

"My gift to you," he said.

"Oh, no, you must have them," I said.

"I have so many. It was a good season."

Gathering up the front of my skirt, I created a fold to carry the apples and accepted them, thanking the archbishop.

He said, "I used to bring Brigid apples as soon as they were ripe. They are quite beneficial to the health. Particularly good for arresting fevers."

I recalled Doctor Symington had said fevers were one of the symptoms Brigid suffered from, thanks to Charles. "You knew my sister well then?"

"We became close friends, yes. She was tireless in trying to help raise money for the cathedral. To show my appreciation, I would come visit her with a basket filled with apples. She and Charles were living in their house on Johnson Street. Sometimes I came by and she'd be sitting in the parlor by the fireplace wrapped in her quilt. I'd place the apples on the hearth to roast. We'd tell each other stories, of our families, of our troubles." He shrugged. "And then, when the apples were ready, I'd take out the little knife I carry with me and carefully peel off the skin. She'd watch me so closely as I did this. And when I was finished, I cut the apple into small slices and fed them to her. She called me the finest cook in Santa Fe."

Yes, he knew of Brigid's illness. Being in his presence, even for these few minutes, I felt a soothing kind of strength from him, coupled with calm. It must have been a tonic for Brigid, as well.

"I should go now," he said. "Please come by next week. I'd enjoy showing you my garden. You can tell me about the life of a new postulant, and I can tell you about growing old in New Mexico."

He laughed. It was a splendid laugh, one that immediately softened the severity of his features, and also revealed the loss of many of his teeth, though he seemed untroubled by it.

\* \* \*

Returning to the house, I saw Mrs. Medrano standing on the back porch, a fretful expression on her face. She said she had grown concerned when I had been gone so long and did not see me down in the garden. "I just asked Mr. Jessup to go look for you," she said.

I apologized for making her worry. I could not blame her for her fears, given what had happened to Brigid. Mr. Jessup came around from the side of the house.

"Good. You're here," he said.

Giving the apples along with the roses I had collected to Mrs. Medrano, I told them of my conversation with Archbishop Lamy, but not of the circumstances leading up to it. It seemed the prudent thing. How could I tell them of this latest incident at the river? They would think me a lunatic. If someone told me of chasing black figures and hearing strange whispers, I might well think the same of them. Yet, I was as certain as I could be about what I had seen and heard. There was a good, sound explanation for all of it. And it would come to me soon enough. It had to. God would see to it.

Mr. Jessup said he could take me to the Spiegelberg store now, if I liked.

"Yes, we should go," I said and adjusted my sister's hat on my head.

The surrey waited at the front of the house. The workmen were still there, sawing and stacking the wood in piles near the side of the house. The hole that remained where the tree had stood had a strange, unsettling appearance, like an unfinished grave.

## Chapter Twenty-Six

In the front window of Mr. Spiegelberg's store stood a mannequin wearing a long cream-colored dress with a high lacey collar. I had seen another of these wax model mannequins back home in a dressmaker's shop window. They were lifelike, yet lifeless. But the dress looked like something Brigid would have worn.

A man in a black coat with a close-cut beard and curly hair appeared in the doorway.

"It is a silk damask gown," he said. "All the way from Paris, France. She wears it well, wouldn't you say?" I recognized the German accent, having heard it many times back in Pittsburgh.

"Yes," I said. "It is beautiful."

Mr. Jessup came up beside me and introduced me to the gentleman, Mr. Willi Spiegelberg.

"Welcome, Miss Danaher," he said and extended his hand to shake mine. "A pleasure to make your acquaintance. Mr. Preston told me to expect you."

I thanked him.

"All of us here so admired your sister," he said. "It was very sad about her passing. She was a true lady, and a good friend."

"I appreciate that, Mr. Spiegelberg."

"It would be my pleasure to assist you today. How can I help?"

161

"I've come because I need some dresses. I may be here in Santa Fe for a while."

"We have dresses for every occasion," he said as he led me into the store. A cavernous place it was, filled with merchandise for every need, at least that I could tell.

He stopped in front of a wall of shelves. Dresses lay folded on them. There were wool, gingham, muslin, calico and linen dresses, and so many colors to choose from.

"There are more in the back if these are not to your liking," he said. "We pride ourselves on having the widest and best selection of merchandise in town. Everything from a pin to a piano."

He had no sooner finished speaking when I had chosen two dark blue wool dresses and a green gingham dress.

"Very good," he said and then asked me if I would like to see some hats. "A new shipment arrived only yesterday. Quite stylish for everyday wear."

I could not fault him for his efforts. Brigid's hat was very plain, but it suited me fine. I told Mr. Spiegelberg I liked my hat, that it had been my sister's.

"Of course," he said with a smile. "I thought I recognized it. But should your mind change, you come back."

He took the dresses from me, and we headed for the counter at the front of the store. Through the front door glass I could see Mr. Jessup waiting outside by the surrey.

Mr. Spiegelberg said, "I know that my wife, Flora, would like to meet you. Perhaps you will come to dinner at our house soon?"

"That sounds very nice, thank you."

"You are from Pittsburgh?"

"I was born there," I said.

"How was your journey to come here?"

I told him it had been long and tiring.

He said, "When I brought my wife here from Europe, it took us many months. That was thirteen years ago. First, we crossed the ocean. Very hard with the seasickness. Then we rode the train from New York City to Colorado, a place called West Los Animas." He shook his head. "This America is a very big country. So many days on the train. My Flora thought we would never get here."

At the counter he drew a sheet of brown paper from a large roll, tore it off and began wrapping my dresses in it.

"And then from West Los Animas to here we rode the stagecoach," he went on. "My Flora said it was terrible. Especially the meals. Bear steaks and buffalo tongues. Flora says never again will she eat a buffalo tongue. Most unfortunate."

"And why is that?" I asked.

"I like buffalo tongue, but she will not allow it in the house," he said.

I could not say I was sorry to have missed an opportunity to eat a buffalo tongue.

"If you don't mind my asking," I said, "has your wife gotten used to life here?"

"Oh, very much so." He said she had started a Hebrew school for girls, the first in Santa Fe. Their two daughters, Betty and Rose, attend her school. "She also teaches sewing and needlework and piano lessons. It's a good life for us here."

He handed me my package and escorted me to the door saying he would have his wife invite me and Matthew and Anne to supper one evening very soon. "My brothers and their families will come, too."

"How many brothers do you have?"

"Seven brothers and three sisters," he said, adding that six of the brothers came to America. The youngest, Abraham, did not come here. He had married and opened a bakery in the town of Cassel in Prussia where their parents had lived.

"And what about your sisters?"

"Eva still lives in Cassel and helps at the bakery. Minna and Hanna are both married and live in Albuquerque. My brother Solomon, the oldest, came over first and wrote telling us of wonderful opportunities here. But he has gone back to Prussia. The doctors said he was very ill, and he decided to return home. And Elias, he died a few years after arriving here."

"I am sorry."

"Thank you," he said, then waved his hand in the air. "But we learned a very good lesson from him."

"Oh?"

"It was night, and he was sleeping. You know these people here, they pile dirt on the flat rooftops of their houses."

I recalled Mrs. Medrano telling me of the custom and felt my stomach begin to tighten.

"The roof of his house, it caved in," he said.

My hand flew to my mouth.

Mr. Spiegelberg continued. "The *vigas*, they call them, to support the ceiling? They broke. The roof of his bedroom, it comes down. He was smothered under all the dirt. Can you imagine such a thing? So, when we built our house, my wife and I insisted on a pitched roof. My brothers and their wives, too. All pitched roofs on their houses."

My Father would have said that Elias must have had some Irish blood in him, for something so calamitous as that could only happen to an Irishman. For myself, Mr. Spiegelberg's story about his brother did not cause me as much distress as I thought it might. A truly a strange feeling. It made me wonder, was I becoming used to this place?

## Chapter Twenty-Seven

Outside Mr. Spiegelberg's store, Mr. Jessup asked if there was anything else I needed to tend to while we were in town. It was already well past time for my mid-morning prayers so I said we should get back to the house. I took comfort in the knowledge that God is both patient and understanding.

As we pulled around the driveway at the house, I was glad to see that the workmen had filled the hole left by the tree. I doubted Charles would even notice the tree was gone.

Starting up the front steps, my package of dresses in hand, I heard the front door open. Mrs. Medrano stood in the doorway, a grave look on her face.

"Matthew is in his room," she said.

"Did something happen? Is he hurt?"

"He was sent home."

"Whatever for?"

"The Brother who brought him gave me this." She handed me a sealed envelope. On it was my name written in a florid hand.

I opened it. Inside was a letter from Brother Butolph, the director of the school. The letter was brief. Matthew had been expelled for fighting. No further explanation was provided.

I showed the letter to Mrs. Medrano. She could scarcely believe it. "He has never been in trouble before."

What had happened I wondered as I knocked on Matthew's door. There was no answer. I turned the knob and opened the door. Matthew sat on his bed, his knees up and head down with his arms wrapped around his legs. The sleeve of his school coat was torn at the shoulder.

"I'd like to talk to you, Matthew," I said.

He turned his head away.

Stepping inside I closed the door. "Can you tell me why you were sent home?"

Still looking away, he shook his head sharply.

"If you tell me what happened, maybe I can help."

He said nothing.

I waited. Perhaps he needed a little more time. Turning to leave, I recalled something I had heard Mother say to Father sometimes on the occasions when they had a disagreement.

"All right, then. I understand," I said. "Young men must sort things out for themselves."

I opened the door and stepped into the hallway. The door was nearly closed when I heard his voice.

"Some... Some of the boys have been saying things."

"What kind of things?" I asked, going back inside.

He pulled his knees up closer.

"What have they said?" I sat on the edge of his bed.

He drew his lips tight. "I don't want to say."

"Some things hurt more than others," I said. "You don't have to tell me. We can talk later if you'd like." I stood and started for the door.

Matthew gave me a furtive glance and tucked his head down. "They... make fun of me and, and try to make me look foolish."

I sat down by him again. "Do you want to tell me what they do?"

He took a deep breath. "Pushing me, trying to trip me to make me

166

fall down. Just so I look silly. One especially has been after me. He does things to me to make the other boys laugh at me. I got tired of taking it, so I hit him."

"It sounds like you probably did the right thing."

His head snapped up, a surprised look on his face. Somehow, I just knew Charles had never told Matthew he did anything right. Ever. Let alone how to deal with bullies, either. And I remembered Mr. Jessup saying that Charles told the boy not to embarrass him by getting into fights.

I asked Matthew to tell me how the fight started. He said that it was in the hallway. "He came up behind me and hit me on the back of my head with a heavy book. He's been doing it for a long time, and I took it. I kept hoping he would stop. Just—. But he didn't. And this time I turned around and punched him in the face. He dropped the book and his nose started bleeding and he came at me, so I hit him again and we started fighting. The other boys were yelling and, and I guess that's when Brother Joseph came out of his classroom and pulled us apart. He took us to Brother Butolph's office."

"Didn't any of the other boys tell him what happened?"

"No!" he snapped. "They all ran when they saw Brother Joseph. They hate me. I'm never going back there."

"But what did Brother Butolph say when you told him about the fight?"

"He didn't believe me."

Surely a mistake had been made. Brother Butolph did not know the full story. I hoped he was a reasonable man, one willing to listen.

I found Mr. Jessup outside cleaning the surrey and said I needed him to take me to Matthew's school as soon as it would be convenient.

"I thought you might, ma'am," he said. "I'll be finished shortly."

Up my room, I washed my face and changed into one of the new

167

wool dresses for I felt a chill in the air. The sleeves were a bit long, but that did not bother me.

I needed God's good and calming grace for the task ahead of me. The full reading of my midmorning prayers would offer me that grace and composure. I sat down in Brigid's rocking chair and opened the Divine Office. The opening prayer was from Psalm thirty-one. I could not help the smile that crept across my face. *Be strong and take heart, all who hope in the Lord.*

# Chapter Twenty-Eight

**M**r. Jessup met me at the front door, looking sheepish. "I didn't realize the time, ma'am."

"What do you mean?"

"They're having their midday meal there at St. Michael's. No point in us getting there for at least another hour."

"Let's go anyway," I said. "I'd rather be there waiting for Brother Butolph. Maybe a good chance of seeing him right away."

We drove past the cathedral and rounded the corner onto Water Street where I saw a part of the town unfamiliar to me. A high *adobe* wall surrounded the entire block on the left. Behind it, at the corner where Water Street met College Street, stood the Academy of Our Lady of Light where Anne attended school. The girls must all be inside having their midday meal, as well, I decided, for the grounds were quiet.

Next to the Academy was the sister's stone chapel with its many Gothic spires pointing toward heaven, and beside it, the convent where the sisters lived. Passing it, I noticed one of the sisters at the corner of the convent's rear balcony. Her face was older. She wore a white apron over the front of her black habit and held a broom in her hands, vigorously beating a rug hanging over the railing. That was a familiar task to me; one I performed weekly back at St. Paul's. Mother Superior said the postulants would do the cleaning and the laundry as part of their first-year duties. I cannot say that I missed those particular chores.

As we crossed the College Street bridge, a wood and rock affair, a cool breeze brushed against my face. Sister Agatha liked to call those soft zephyrs God's own tonic. However, I could not resist a look up the river toward Charles's property, to see if that wretch in black was prowling about. I saw only the trees along the riverbank and heard the rustling of their leaves as that breeze continued its soothing touch when a jolt struck the surrey, pitching me to one side, followed by another jolt. I seized the back of the driver's seat to steady myself.

"Beg your pardon, ma'am," Mr. Jessup said. "The wheels dropped into a hole in the planks."

"Clearly a treacherous spot," I said.

"Yes, ma'am. That's the first time I didn't miss it. City ought to fix it, though."

Once off the bridge, the hard dusty road made a steady climb to St. Michael's College at the top of the rise. Three stories tall and long as a city block, there was true grandness to it, though that was tempered for not a single tree or shrub grew nearby.

Nestled beside it, equally impossible to miss but much sadder by far, was the San Miguel chapel. The smooth finish covering the *adobe* walls of the school stood in stark contrast to the precarious nature of the weathered chapel walls, for the mortar between those old and crumbling bricks seemed all but worn away. Half the buttresses along the flat rooftop were already missing. My Father would have said the only thing keeping the chapel standing was God Himself.

"Sorrowful looking, isn't it?" Mr. Jessup said as we drew closer.

"Indeed, it is."

"The Indians tried to burn it down once."

"No!" I said, horrified.

"The wooden roof went up fast. They tried burning the whole town, except *adobe* doesn't burn."

"Good Lord. When did this happen?"

"Oh, a long time ago. Before my grandfather's grandfather was Matthew's age. The Indians drove the *Diegos* out. The Indians, they ran them all the way down to the Rio Grande. I hear some Indians wished they'd run them back to Spain. But they came back some years later, made peace with the Indians. Been here ever since."

"But why did the Indians do such a thing? Try to burn everything down?"

"Didn't much like the *Diego* boys. That's what I was told anyway."

It seemed clear to me Mr. Jessup was determined to continue to call any foreigner by some disparaging name, and I was just as determined to continue to ask God to show him we are all made in His image. But my prayers had yet gone unanswered. I took some solace in believing God had His reasons.

A rough *adobe* wall too high to see over surrounded the courtyard of the chapel. One of the two doors of the gateway stood open. White crosses were scattered about the inside of the courtyard. Mr. Jessup said most of them marked the graves of the Franciscan friars, Spanish soldiers and Christian Indians who built the chapel. He abruptly reined the horses to stop by the gate.

"Is something the matter?" I asked.

"No ma'am. Mrs. Medrano mentioned that she told you about the old bell. Now I know you've got matters to address, but Brother Butolph's not going anywhere and it's not often the gate is open."

A few more minutes shouldn't make any difference, I decided. And I was curious about this St. Joseph Bell that Mrs. Medrano had said sounded like the angels singing.

"We don't need to go in," I said, believing it would save some time.

"Look here," Mr. Jessup said, "by the corner of the chapel."

Seeing it nearly broke my heart. Dingy and dirty, the coppery-colored bell lay on its side. A good-sized bell, I guessed it was nearly as tall as Anne. And it appeared to have sunken into the ground some. No doubt from being such a heavy thing.

"It must have been terrible," I said.

"Ma'am?"

"The storm. Mrs. Medrano said it blew the tower down.

Mr. Jessup grunted. "That storm might have helped it along."

I asked him what he meant.

He said a stonemason who worked on the cathedral had told him that the belfry the old friars had built was not nearly strong enough.

"What do you mean not strong enough?"

"Too much bell for the tower," he said. "It weighs seven hundred pounds. Every time they rang it, the tower walls got a little bit weaker. And they pulled the rope to ring it every day for a lot of years."

"Well, they ought not to leave it in the dirt that way. Lying there twelve years. It's shameful."

"I agree," came a voice from the other side of the wall, startling me. A priest dressed in a long black cassock stepped out into the open gateway, wiping his hands with a rag. He wore spectacles and had dark rumpled hair.

"You gave me a fright, father," I said.

"I apologize," he said. "I was oiling the hinges on the gate and couldn't help overhearing you. I'm Father Dominic."

I introduced Mr. Jessup and myself. "Is this your chapel then?" I asked.

"It is," he said. "And Mr. Jessup, you're close. The bell weighs seven hundred and eighty pounds. You know, some say angels came down and carried it to the ground during that storm to protect it from harm, but I say the graves saved it."

"The graves?" Mr. Jessup said in a dubious tone.

Father Dominic nodded. "I believe a couple of the graves here in the courtyard broke the bell's fall. When it hit the ground, the coffins buried here probably collapsed under the dirt from the weight. I've looked the bell over and there's not a mark or a crack to be found. I keep praying we'll have the money someday to rebuild the tower."

"Lack of money is the reason they have for most everything that can't get done around here," Mr. Jessup said.

"Sad but true," Father Dominic said. "Would you care to come in and see the bell?"

I admit I was tempted, but I begged off, telling him another time, perhaps. And though Matthew's situation needed my attention, I could not ignore the deplorable situation with the bell and the words were out of my mouth. "I don't mean to sound impertinent, father, but surely the archbishop could help with repairs and getting the bell back where it belongs."

"I'm afraid he cannot."

"But why?"

"When he invited the Christian Brothers to come here and start a school, he donated this land and the chapel to them so they could accomplish that task. It all belongs to them. They built St. Michael's with the understanding it would have to support itself. The money to do that comes from tuition and some donations. The Sisters of Loretto face the same obligations. The archbishop donated land to them, as well, to build their academy and chapel. Of course, their chapel is only a few years old. San Miguel chapel has been here for two hundred years. And the cost of running St. Michael's doesn't leave much left over to put a new tower on this old chapel to hang a very heavy bell."

"What about taking up a second collection at Sunday Mass?" I asked.

He smiled wryly. "Only the Brothers and the boys who board here attend this chapel. That was part of the understanding between the archbishop and the Brothers. The boys and the Brothers are my flock, my congregation. That doesn't put much in the collection basket Sunday mornings."

"Father Dominic?"

We looked back toward the chapel. A ruddy-faced Brother stood there. He wore the black tunic and the stiff white collar split in the middle called a rabat that all the Brothers wore.

"Is it time already, Brother Ephrem?" Father Dominic asked.

The Brother nodded.

"Take them inside," Father Dominic said. "I'll be along in a moment."

Brother Ephrem ushered a line of boys, dressed in their coats, out the side door of the school building and into the chapel.

"I must go hear confessions," Father Dominic said to us as he stepped back to close the doors.

"Thank you for your kindness," I said. "And I hope someday the bell has a strong tower to ring from. I'm told it sounds like the singing of the angels."

He held the door open. "It's a funny thing, Miss Danaher. Some people tell me they've heard the bell peal late at night sometimes."

"Do they now," I said.

"It's not possible, of course," he went on. "But I don't try to convince them otherwise. It brings them comfort, I suppose."

He closed the doors and a loud clang followed as he threw the latch locking them.

Mr. Jessup grunted.

"Something on your mind, Mr. Jessup?"

"It strikes me as a little strange what people think they hear sometimes. Bells that can't ring. Awfully strange."

I was not about to tell him of the whispers I'd heard, let alone what I'd encountered, earlier this morning. Besides, I had pressing matters to tend to with Brother Butolph.

# Chapter Twenty-Nine

"Come with me, please. Brother Butolph will see you now," the Brother said. He was a young man with a closely cropped beard and uneven eyes in his face.

I had been waiting better than twenty minutes. But I did not complain. Besides, it had given me time to consider the situation further, and to say a prayer.

Following the Brother down the long hallway, I noticed a couple of boys peek from around a corner. The Brother clapped his hands sharply. The boys snapped their heads back, and the sound of running feet echoed.

On the wall behind Brother Butolph's desk hung a framed portrait of John Baptiste de La Salle, the founder of the Christian Brothers order. From the picture of the man, La Salle struck me as a kindly sort, for he possessed caring eyes and the hint of a smile.

Brother Butolph was altogether different. His eyes were deep set and hard, and his mouth curled in a way I can only describe as disapproving. So set was his grim visage, I could not help but wonder if he ever smiled.

He indicated the chair across from his desk and invited me to sit down. I detected only a slight German accent when he spoke. And there was an almost soothing quality in Brother Butolph's voice. Almost.

I thanked him for seeing me and before I could say another word, he asked me if I had come about Matthew.

When I said I had, he said, "Matthew is expelled. It was in the letter I sent you. Is there anything else, Miss Danaher?"

It was obvious he was not about to yield on Matthew's expulsion. And neither was I.

"Perhaps there are some things you're not aware of," I said.

"If you wish," he said.

Relating the story Matthew had told me of the incident with the other boy, I concluded stating the fight started when the boy struck Matthew in the back of the head with the book. "That boy had done this numerous times before to Matthew," I said. "Matthew didn't start the fight. But he did finish it. I don't see how he can be faulted for that."

"I spoke with three boys," Brother Butolph said. "They all agree Matthew was the instigator."

I knew well that some of my girls at St. Paul's would defend a friend no matter what the instance. As admirable a trait as that was, I told my girls that truth was always the better path. "These boys," I said, "are they friends of the one who struck Matthew?"

"I think more to the point is that Matthew has been involved in several other altercations."

"You mean more fights?"

He nodded. "With other boys in the past few weeks."

"That would be since his Mother's attack."

"I'm afraid so, yes. I took that into account, but enough is enough."

"Do you know what those other boys did to provoke Matthew?"

"I'm not aware that they provoked him at all."

"Did you ask them?"

"Of course."

"And are these boys always truthful?"

He slowly sat back in his chair and pursed his thin lips, joined his hands, and tapped his thumbs together. I could see in his eyes he was taking the measure of me. Had he found my question insolent? Or was it my willfulness that Mother Superior warned me to curb that he saw? Had I caught him in a lie, or perhaps trying to hide something? It made little difference. I concluded his purpose was to intimidate me, to stare me down. Well, I was my Mother's daughter and proud of it I was. I fixed my eyes on his. I would wait him out.

"We accept all kinds of boys here," he finally said. "Boys from prominent families and boys from meager means. American boys, Mexican boys, Indians. We have clever boys eager to learn and those needing more attention. Some families can pay the tuition. Some cannot. We make allowances because we are here to educate, to instill in them the word of God. What we do not have here are boys who disrupt our efforts and our rules. Matthew is expelled. That is final. Good day, Miss Danaher."

The man had made up his mind. Any further discussion was fruitless for facts would have only confused him.

Was I angry? Indeed, I was. But my immediate concern now was to make Charles aware of this situation. In spite of his edict that all matters were left to me to resolve in his absence, and in spite of my own feelings about him, Charles needed to be told. It was the right thing and the proper thing to do.

The problem I faced was that I did not know where to reach Charles. While he no doubt believed he had thought of everything, he had either forgotten or intentionally left me no address as to where he would be staying in Denver. That presented only one alternative to me, and that was to go see his business partner. I asked Mr. Jessup to take me to Mr. Catron's office.

"I wish things had gone better for you," Mr. Jessup said as we drove toward the bridge. "Brother Butolph is one hard-headed Dutchy. I mean German, ma'am."

Perhaps my prayers for Mr. Jessup were working and he was changing his ways a little.

"We'll find an answer, Mr. Jessup, with God's help."

"Yes, ma'am."

I could not disagree with Mr. Jessup's assessment of Brother Butolph's temperament. And I hoped Mr. Catron was not the pompous vermin that Charles was, but my more immediate concern was that Mr. Catron would be able to see me. He would have to see me. A sudden chill swept over me. Deep it went, like an icy river running through my bones. As quickly as it came, it vanished. And it was then I realized we were crossing the bridge. A raven sat perched on the wooden railing close by. It shook its feathers then opened it wings and swooped underneath the bridge and I heard those strange words again in that unsettling whisper.

"Tray may meese he ohz."

I looked about anxiously, for I was certain the black veiled wretch must be nearby, attempting to play another devilish trick on me.

Mr. Jessup showed no indication he heard the awful whispering.

A second time I heard it, goading me. "Tray may meese he ohz."

Come out, you coward! I wanted to shout. And there it was, the black wretch coming up from the riverbank at the end of the bridge. Its back was to me, but I recognized the long black clothes and the black veil covering its head. It reached out a bony hand and took hold of a wooden pillar at the bridge corner, lifting itself to the roadside.

"Stop!" I cried, determined this devil would not escape me again.

All in the same instant Mr. Jessup pulled back hard on the reins as I leapt from the surrey and the wretch halted, cringing on the spot. Its black robed arm was nearly in my grasp. It turned on me and I saw the frightened face of the old sister from the convent, the one I had seen earlier beating the rug on the balcony.

"Oh, forgive me, sister," I said. "I, I thought you were— I'm so sorry." My face burned with humiliation.

"You nearly scared the life out of me," she said, trying to regain her breath. "I go out to take a walk along the river... Every day I take a..."

"Please. I'm very sorry. Are you all right?"

"I believe so," she said, fanning her face with her hand. "Just be more careful, child."

"Yes. I... thank you, sister." I climbed back into the surrey. I could not look at Mr. Jessup.

The old sister hurried down the road toward the convent.

Mr. Jessup turned to me. "I thought you were going to harm that poor woman. What were you thinking, ma'am?"

"I... I thought she..." I calmed myself. "Everything is fine, Mr. Jessup."

I heard a gurgling croak and looked up. A black raven circled lazily overhead. Its deep croak became shriller and grating. A mocking laugh it was.

"Well," Mr. Jessup said, "perhaps I should take you back to the house."

"No. Take me to Mr. Catron."

# Chapter Thirty

On the *plaza*, men on ladders strung lines from truncated tree to truncated tree. They crisscrossed the lines, going from one end of the square to the other. Mr. Jessup said they were preparing for the festivities the next night.

"Festivities?" I asked.

"The Feast of St. Francis of Assisi," he said.

"Oh, yes. I remember now."

He stopped the surrey in front of the building where Mr. Catron had his office. Reaching down by his seat, he brought up his canteen and silver cup and offered me some water.

Still feeling somewhat flustered from my encounter at the bridge, I thanked him and took a sip. It tasted cool and refreshing, though I almost wished he had some of Mrs. Medrano's special brandy with him.

"You going to be all right, ma'am?" he asked.

I nodded and handed him the cup. "This cannot wait."

Mr. Catron's office was at the top of the stairs. His name was painted in black letters on the beveled glass door panel. Looking at it, I could not help recalling all the terrible things Sheriff Martínez had said about Mr. Catron, calling him a thief and claiming he ordered men murdered. Well, whether I liked it or not, I had nowhere else to turn. It was imperative that I contact Charles. Closing my eyes, I asked God for His help, and also to keep me safe. I knocked on the glass. A woman's voice told me to come in.

Opening the door, I saw a woman with flaxen hair standing on a ladder. She was pulling a thick law book from a high shelf. Every wall was covered by bookshelves, and every shelf was full of books.

"Just a moment, please," she said, climbing down the ladder. She set the book on a long table covered with stacks of paper. "Yes, how can I help you?"

"I'd like to see Mr. Catron, please, if he's about," I said.

"And whom shall I say wants to see him?"

"My name is Catherine Danaher."

"Ah, Miss Danaher, welcome," she said, and another voice boomed from the far corner of the office where windows nearly met. "Come in, Miss Danaher."

In that corner behind the large desk was a great chair with its back to the room. Like a throne it seemed to me. It swiveled around and the man seated in it set aside papers he held in his hands and rose up from the chair.

"I'm Thomas Catron," he said. "I've been looking forward to making your acquaintance."

His presence could put a palpable fear into a person. A towering giant of porcine girth with sagging jowls and a thick moustache salted with flecks of grey, he wore a dark coat and a white shirt with a stiff collar and black bow tie around his thick neck.

Offering his hand, I shook it. I noted the fierceness in his sharp, pale eyes. A viable asset for an attorney, for I could see at once they were forceful enough to weaken an opponent's resolve.

"It's a pleasure to have you here," he said, his thunderous voice having quieted to a soft rumble, and pulled out a chair for me to sit down. "What can I do for you?"

I told him of Matthew's predicament and of my meeting with Brother Butolph. "I must send Charles a telegram immediately. He should be made aware of the situation."

"And indeed, he shall," he said. "I'll see to it personally." He turned to his secretary. "Miss Warren, paper and a pen for Miss Danaher, please."

She handed them to me with a reassuring smile.

"He's staying at the Windsor Hotel in Denver," he told me. "Please write down your message. I'll add my own urgency to it."

I wrote that Matthew had been expelled and that a new school must be found for him immediately.

Mr. Catron took the paper. "Fine. As soon as he responds with an answer, I'll come out to the house personally and let you know. We'll see to it this situation gets resolved."

I thanked him.

As we left the *plaza*, I told Mr. Jessup that I thought Mr. Catron a very sincere and helpful man. "His concern appeared quite genuine. Not a devil at all."

"Yes, ma'am," he said.

I thought I heard him mumble something else, but perhaps not.

# Chapter Thirty-One

Returning to the house, I told Mrs. Medrano of the episode with Brother Butolph and of Mr. Catron's offer of help with the matter. I asked her about other schools that Matthew might attend. She said there were no other Catholic boys' schools in Santa Fe. There was a Protestant school in town run by the Presbyterians but that was out of the question. The Jesuits had opened a school in Albuquerque, and there was a Catholic school in Colorado in the town of Trinidad. I did not like the sound of those, either, for they would take him away from home and that was not why I was brought here. Perhaps there were other possibilities. Maybe I could take over his schooling. We would have to see.

"How is Matthew?" I asked.

"He's up in his room. Reading."

"Is he now."

Ascending the stairs, I expected to find him with Mr. Fairchild's volume clutched in his hands.

The first thing I noticed on entering his room was that he'd straightened things up. Clothes and toys were put away. His bed was made. As for Matthew, he sat reading. It looked like it was one of his schoolbooks. Not being at all sure what to say now, I asked him how he was feeling.

"Good," he said and set down his book. "I'm sorry about being expelled. I know that's a bad thing. I've caused problems."

The guilt on his face was as plain as could be.

"We'll get them straightened out," I said. "What are you reading there?"

"My English composition book. I need to try to keep up with my lessons. Mother told Anne and me we need to use the brains God gave us. She said they are a blessing."

The very words Mother gave to Brigid and me.

"I'll leave you to it, then," I said.

Whatever the outcome of this predicament, I knew in my heart Matthew would come through it.

Of course, Anne needed to be told. I was in my room reading my mid-afternoon prayers when Mrs. Medrano knocked at the door. She said Mr. Jessup had brought Anne home and she wanted to see me. "She knows about Matthew."

"I thought we all agreed I would be the one to tell her," I said.

She said Anne heard it from Matthew. "When Mr. Jessup did not get him from school after getting her, she knew something was the matter."

Anne was waiting by her bedroom door as I came out. She ran to me, tears welling in her eyes. Taking her into my room, we sat in the rocking chair, Anne on my lap.

"Is Matthew going away?" she asked.

"And why should he do that?"

"Father told us we had to be good after Mother died. If we weren't, he said he'd send us away."

"He did, did he?" A fine thing, threatening his children with banishment.

She nodded, wiping her eyes.

"And did he tell you where he'd send you?"

"To school, in the east someplace. And, and Matthew is in trouble and Father will send him away. I don't want him to go." Tears ran down her cheeks.

I held her close. What to say to her? The truth was best, at least as far as I knew it to be.

"No one is going anywhere," I said. "Not if I can help it."

# Chapter Thirty-Two

After the children had said their prayers and I put them to bed, Mrs. Medrano told me she was going to brew some tea and would I care for a cup. I asked if she was adding that special brandy of hers to it. She said she was, and I gladly accepted.

We went to the tower sitting room to enjoy our tea. I saw the moon rising in all its bright fullness through one of the windows as we sat quietly for a bit. The silence was as calming as the tea. And as often happens, the incidents of the day passed through my mind, and I mentioned to Mrs. Medrano that I had heard the strangest thing.

"I think the words were Spanish, but I don't know," I said.

"Do you remember them?"

"It sounded something like tray may meese he ohz."

Mrs. Medrano's face turned pale. "Where did you hear that?"

"When I was in the garden this morning, and again when Mr. Jessup took me across the river."

"Did you see who said it?"

I did not want to have to explain my unfortunate pursuit of the scoundrel in black that led to my near collision with Archbishop Lamy, nor the whole embarrassing incident with the old sister. "I only heard it," I said.

"Did Mr. Jessup hear it?"

"I don't think so."

Medrano spoke in Spanish. "*Tráeme mis hijos.*"

"Yes. That was it."

"You are certain that is what you heard?"

"I am. What does it mean?"

She let out a haggard sigh. "It means bring me my children."

"I don't understand."

"It is a warning."

"A warning? For what?"

She sat there, trembling, her cup shaking in her hands. Something genuinely frightened her.

I set down my cup. "Mrs. Medrano?"

"I must tell you something," she said, fear in her eyes. "It will not be easy for you to hear, but you must listen."

"All right. Tell me."

"I must start at the beginning. Many, many years ago, a beautiful girl lived here named Maria. Her family was poor. Men came asking her to marry, but she refused because she wanted only to marry a rich and handsome man. One day, she saw such a man, the son of one of the wealthiest families in Santa Fe and she made certain that he saw her. And when he did, it was as though he was struck by a thunderbolt. They married and lived in a big house, and she wore only beautiful clothes. Soon she gave him two children, a boy and a girl. But after a few years, Maria's husband no longer cared for her and before long he came home less and less.

"One evening, Maria was on the *plaza* with the children. Her husband drove by them in a big carriage. Sitting beside him was another woman, very beautiful and very young. Maria called to him, but he laughed and drove on. It broke something inside her. She took her children to the river and threw them in, and they drowned."

I gasped, bringing my hand to my mouth.

"Being rid of the children she thought she could win her husband back," Mrs. Medrano continued. "But when she saw what she had done, she jumped into the river to try to save them, and she drowned. At the gates of Heaven, God asked Maria, 'Where are your children?' She said she did not know. But God saw in her face that she was lying. To punish her for her sins, He put a mark on her face like Cain and condemned her to search the river each night looking for her lost children. She cries and calls out, '¿Dónde están mis hijos?' It means, where are my children? And, 'Tráeme mis hijos.' Bring me my children."

"You're telling me this is the woman I heard?"

"Please. Let me finish. She tries to lure the children of others to the river to drown them so they can take the place of her own dead children. She is called *La Llorona*."

"What does that mean?"

"The Weeping Woman."

Oh, good Lord, I thought.

"They say if you hear *La Llorona* you are *maldito*," she said. "Cursed."

*Maldito*. The word I had heard in the garden that morning. "Mrs. Medrano, I don't believe in curses and for all I know it was some rascal playing a joke on me before."

"I hope you are right," she said. "But the curse, it is real."

Now I was curious. "What is this curse?"

"They say if you hear the cries of *La Llorona*, you or someone close to you will soon die."

There it was. The tale of the banshee. I was ready to tell her of it, I wanted to, but I could see how much this story had upset her.

"Do many people know about this Weeping Woman?" I asked.

"Everyone has heard the story."

So, the black wretch at the river was some scoundrel after all trying to frighten me. At least that was cleared up now.

"But not everyone believes," Mrs. Medrano went on. "*La Llorona* has been seen many times by the river, but I have heard people say they have seen her on the road or by their own houses. Other places."

"So, it's arbitrary, then."

She gave me a questioning look.

"She appears by chance," I said.

"She comes when she comes. But I know the river. It is not safe."

I remembered the other day when Mr. Jessup took me to the cemetery to see my sister's grave there was a funeral procession for two children. I told Mrs. Medrano that Mr. Jessup had said the children being buried had drowned in the river. "He said he read about it in the newspaper. But he didn't say this crying woman drowned them."

She drew her lips tight. "*Sí*. It was *La Llorona*."

"How can you be so sure? The newspaper didn't..." I stopped speaking as I saw Mrs. Medrano staring into her cup, a fearful look in her eyes.

"Mrs. Medrano?"

In a small voice she said, "Some say Mrs. Preston was drowned by *La Llorona*."

Had I heard her right? "What did you say?"

"I am not saying it is true, but she was at the river that night and maybe she saw *La Llorona* trying to pull a child into the water or, or maybe *La Llorona* was—"

"Stop it! My sister was not killed by a, a ghost story."

"Forgive me, please. I did not mean to give offense."

"And I didn't mean to be so sharp with you," I said, calming myself down. "I'm sorry. But I find all this so, so unbelievable."

She set her cup aside. "There was a boy many years ago. He was about Matthew's age. He went..." She glanced down.

"Mrs. Medrano, I—"

"*Por favor*. Please. I must tell you. He went to the river one night. His *mamá* and *papá* had warned him never to go, but his friends dared him. They told him to go to the dead tree by the river and stay there until midnight. They said he was a coward if he did not. When he got to the river he heard a strange sound, like the crying of a baby, but it turned to shrieks. The terrible sound was all around him. Something very cold struck him, and he fell down. He felt blood on his face. He looked up and saw a woman with a face like a skull and dressed in a torn black shroud standing over him. She screamed, '¡*Venga conmigo!* Come with me!'

"The boy was so scared. He got to his feet and ran, but *La Llorona* caught him and dragged him past the tree to the river. She rose up into the air, holding him by his arms. He shut his eyes tight, certain he would be thrown into the water and drowned. He prayed to God to save him, and he heard the bell of San Miguel chapel begin to ring very loudly. Then a terrible loud cry filled his ears, a wailing too awful to describe, and suddenly, the boy felt himself falling and he struck the ground hard, almost knocking the wind from his lungs. He tried to catch his breath. He thought *La Llorona* was coming back for him, but she was gone. Disappeared. When he came home, he told his parents what had happened. They were very angry with him for being so foolish and his *papá* took off his belt to beat him. But his *mamá*, she saw his face was scratched, like fingernails had cut his cheeks, and his clothes were torn and bloody. She knew *La Llorona* had done this to him."

I thought this story pure folly. And it obviously had nothing to do with Brigid. It was a tale told by parents to scare their children and make them behave. I asked Mrs. Medrano about the church bell, and she said the only time the bell was rung was to announce the start of the Mass.

"Was there a Mass that night?" I asked.

"No," she said, "but the priest, he was asleep in his room at the chapel when he heard the bell ringing. He went to see if someone had broken in to play a trick on him, but the doors were bolted shut. He looked up where the bell rope hung. The bell was ringing over and over, he said, but no one was pulling the rope."

"Maybe it was the wind."

"You know about the bell. It is too heavy for the wind."

"Well, someone was ringing that bell."

"*Sí.* God, or maybe one of His angels." She crossed herself. "But that boy, he was saved from *La Llorona.*"

"I know you believe this story but—"

"The boy was my son."

A mother's love made this a much thornier matter. But I needed to address this in the gentlest way to say what I needed to say. "Mrs. Medrano, I'm trying to understand, but I have to wonder, is it possible your son might have torn his own clothes and scratched his face himself so you wouldn't punish him for disobeying you?"

She shook her head. "When he got home and told us what happened, the words fell from his mouth, like crazy talk. And his eyes, they stared at nothing. When I saw the scratches and the blood on his face, I tell you, I was too scared to move. My husband and me, we thought he would never be the same. It was only by the grace of God that we were not struck by the curse."

"And why was that?" I asked.

"Because my son devoted his life to God. He became a priest."

Mrs. Medrano went on talking, something about the river and

Charles's property, but I was not listening. I was not about to argue with her over the reason for her son's decision to join the priesthood. Something had put a terrible fright into him. That was clear enough. But I could not accept the outlandish story about this crying woman, this river ghost. It was no more real than the banshee or the death coach or any of the other ghostly tales my Father told me.

"The tree."

"Pardon me?" I said.

Mrs. Medrano was now standing over by the window facing the back of the property.

"Please," she said, motioning to me to join her. She pointed, beyond the house and past the garden, at the ugly dead tree at the river's edge, bright in the moonlight with its one gnarled branch jutting up into the night. "That is what worried me so when Mr. Preston told us he bought this land to build a big house on."

"But it's only a dead tree."

She shook her head. "That is where *La Llorona* is said to have drowned her two children. Mrs. Preston was found in the river by it. Those waters are cursed."

# Chapter Thirty-Three

I woke from a fitful sleep when I heard the woman whisper. Her thin voice sounded so close.

"*Tráeme mis hijos.*"

The candle burning in the holding dish on the stand next to my bed was almost a yellow puddle. The flame struggled to remain lit.

"*Tráeme mis hijos.*"

Sitting up in bed, I took the candle and held it out before me. In the dimming glow, things appeared in order. No rustling of the curtains. No items rearranged. No sign of the wretch in black. Wait! My door was open. How had that happened? And there, in the shadow by the corner of the armoire, did something move?

"Aunt Catherine?"

A gasp escaped my lips.

Anne and Matthew stood in the bedroom doorway. Candlelight flickered from the chandelier hanging behind them above the landing.

"Children, what are you doing up?" I asked, and every candle flame in the chandelier quivered then vanished in the same instant, even the flame of the candle in my hand.

"I'm scared," Anne whimpered.

"Come here quickly." I held open my arms.

The whole house had gone dark. I could see nothing. No light penetrated from outside. No moonlight. It was as though we had disappeared into the void, and we were all that remained in the thick darkness.

The room felt brutally cold, and I held the children close. Anne curled beside me with her arms about my waist and her face buried in the folds of my nightdress. Matthew was lodged on the other side of me, his hand clasping mine. Scared he was, for his hand was cold and clammy. Our shallow breaths and the rapid beating of our hearts was all I could hear.

"Do not move," I whispered. "Do not make a sound."

I heard something moving. Where was it? I strained to see through the black darkness. Something was near. But where? A voice whispered. Anne? No. It was outside the room. I heard it again. What was it saying? I turned my head to listen closer. It stopped, the silence as heavy as the dark. I sat still, almost afraid to move. Something was there. A sound. Soft. Familiar. My door. It had closed shut! But what had closed it?

Matthew gripped my hand. It will be all right I wanted to say. Anne trembled against my leg. Matthew squeezed my hand harder. I tried to loosen his grip, to pull my hand free, but he held it fast. I nearly cried out from the pain, for it felt as though my hand was being crushed in a vise. Let go of my hand, I wanted to cry out.

A faint breath brushed my cheek, and I was aware of a foul moldy smell.

"Stay close, children," I whispered then I felt Anne struggle against me.

"Mama is out there!" she screamed.

"Anne, stop!" I said.

"Mama is calling us!" Matthew cried.

"No!" I said. "It's not her!"

"It is!" Anne cried. "I hear her. She says to come and play. Come

195

and play children!"

"No!" I held her tightly.

"Let me go!" She struggled harder to pull away from me.

"It's not her!" I said.

"It is!" Matthew shouted.

"No! It's a trick!" I held them fast.

"*¡Tráeme mis hijos!*"

Was the wretch in my room?

"It's mama, it's mama." Anne screamed. "Let me go!"

"Bring me my children!" the voice cried.

I heard Mr. Fairchild's voice shout, "Beware the river!"

A cacophony of shouts and murmurs descended. "Bring me my children!" "Beware the river!" "Cursed." "*¿Dónde están mis hijos?*" "*Maldito.*" "Bring me my children!" "Beware the river!" "Catherine! Bring them to me!"

Oh, my God! It knows my name!

A great blow sounded from somewhere downstairs.

The children became rigid beside me. I could not move.

Another blow sounded, louder, stronger. It was at the front door. More blows struck, each more vehement than the last. It wanted inside. Another mighty blow fell, then a long maddening groan and the sound of wood snapping and breaking.

The children screamed. I felt Anne hold me tighter.

One more great blow battered against the door. A loud sickening thud followed, the door crashing to the floor. The malignant thing was in the house! A horrid shrieking rushed up the stairs. The thing pounded at my door, thundering and furious! The hinges moaned. The door protruded inward, the monstrous force pressing against it.

"Bring me my children!" screamed the voice beyond the door.

"Hail Mary, full of grace," I prayed. "Hail Mary, full of grace."

"*¡Senorita!*" It was Mrs. Medrano! She was out there in the hallway! "Go back!" I shouted. "Get away!"

The fierce pounding on the door increased, the wood cracking and splintering under the assault.

"*¡Senorita!* Where are you?"

"Catherine! Bring me my children!"

There was a terrible strangled scream, and I woke, startled and damp with sweat. Was that my scream I'd heard?

The candle by my bed was nearly out. Quiet enveloped the house. The only sound was my shallow breathing. Shadows remained still. The door stood closed and snug on its hinges.

I sensed the presence of arms about my waist. My left hand felt as though squeezed in a vice. The children! But they were not there. I raised my left hand up to my face. My red and throbbing fingers were squeezed tightly together. Good Lord, had I done this to myself?

# Chapter Thirty-Four

Unable to sleep, I lay in my bed, praying for God's grace, trying not to think about that terrible nightmare, trying to banish all thoughts of this Weeping Woman from my mind, and trying not to look into the deep shadows lurking about the room.

With the dawn I rose from my bed and got down on my knees, opened the Divine Office and prayed my first daily prayers. But those disquieting memories persisted. Surely that awful dream was the result of drinking Mrs. Medrano's special brandy mixed with my tea. How could I believe some sobbing woman prowled the river? Or of bells ringing by themselves? These stories were absurd, weren't they? And Brigid's body found by the dead tree was but coincidence, wasn't it?

Oh, this place! This confounding upside down place! There had to be someone I could—

A noise downstairs startled me, and I realized it must be Mrs. Medrano going out to the kitchen to prepare breakfast. The children would be up soon.

I dressed and kissed my Mother's crucifix. Opening the curtains, light streamed into the room. The day appeared glorious. No dead swathes covered the garden. No sign of the black wretch skulking by the river. But someone wearing a straw hat and blue work shirt and carrying a bucket of water was walking up from the river through the garden. I was about to throw open the window and call out when the man raised his head, and I recognized the old archbishop. He waved and motioned with his hand to come around to the front of the house.

Descending the stairs, I went out the front door and found him slowly emptying the water into a fresh bed of dirt surrounding a new seedling tree planted close by where the old cottonwood had fallen.

"Your Excellency?" I asked.

He looked up, a tired smile on his dirt-smudged face. "Good day, *mademoiselle*. I thought an elm might go well here. A good shade tree in the summer months."

His voice sounded oddly muted. The poor man had caught a cold.

"That's very generous of you, Excellency, but you needn't have. Especially since you're fighting a cold."

"It is my pleasure." He set down the bucket. "And my cold is only temporary."

I invited him inside. "A cup of tea. Or breakfast. It wouldn't be any trouble, I'm sure."

"That is tempting, but no thank you." He lowered his voice. "Please, tell me, how is Matthew?"

He must have heard about the expulsion. I told him Matthew was doing well, all things considered, and that I was waiting to hear from Charles about finding a new school.

"Well, Matthew is a good lad." He quickly pulled a handkerchief from his pocket and covered his nose as he sneezed. "And give Brother Butolph some time. He's a practical man."

Had he spoken with the Brother? I wanted to ask but felt it would have been wrong. But perhaps there was something else I could ask him about.

"I'm not finished, you know," I heard him say.

I frowned. The newly planted elm looked sturdy enough to me. "Excellency?"

"My work here," he said, looking about with a longing in his eyes. "The cathedral, my garden. My hopes. So much left to do." He sighed. "I resisted for many years, but I have come to accept that much of life is but unfinished business. But not this night, *mademoiselle*." A smile spread across his face. "This is the eve of the feast of St. Francis of Assisi, and I have much still to prepare for tonight's celebration."

I could not help myself. The words flew from my mouth. "I need to ask you for your guidance on a matter, if I may."

"Of course, child. If I can."

"I have heard a story, about the Weeping Woman."

"Ah, *La Llorona*," he said ruefully.

"So, there is no truth to it?"

"These are good people here, but many of them believe in silly superstitions. This *La Llorona* is one they use to frighten their children. In France, parents tell us fairy tales like *Le Petit Chaperon Rouge*. You know it. Little Red Riding Hood."

"Of course."

"But it was not told to frighten us. It was to teach us a lesson. To never trust a stranger, for wolves may lurk in every guise. But this crying woman." He shook his head wearily.

"Do you believe there was such a woman who drowned her own children?"

"I don't know. But they believe it." He cocked his head at me. "Don't tell me you accept this nonsense."

My anxiety must have shown on my face.

"No, no," I said. "It's just been a very trying few days." His words had relieved my apprehensions considerably.

"Hello, children," he called out.

I turned and saw Matthew and Anne peeking from around the front door.

"Good morning, Your Excellency," they said.

Mrs. Medrano appeared and greeted the archbishop. "I'm sorry," she said. "They heard voices and became curious."

"Curiosity is a good thing in moderation," he said.

She whispered to the children and ushered them back inside.

After a moment he looked at me and said, "Your sister was a good woman."

A sudden pang grew in my chest.

He went on. "She raised two fine children. They will," he thought a moment, as though searching for the right word, "endure."

"You're most kind, Excellency. Thank you."

He told me he hoped to see all of us at the celebration that night and started off down the driveway, his bucket in one hand and his shovel over his shoulder. He suddenly stopped and turned. "I will tell you this," he said, "if there truly was a woman as they say who murdered her children for the sake of her own selfish happiness, she is damned. And if she drags innocent children to the river to drown them for their souls, she is evil."

# Chapter Thirty-Five

"Mr. Catron is here to see you," Mrs. Medrano said. I was in the tower sitting room, attentive to Matthew, having decided to see to his schooling until other arrangements could be made. He was about to begin a recitation from *David Copperfield* as part of his reading lesson. I had discovered the volume, along with several others of Dickens's works, in a secluded corner of my brother-in-law's study.

Matthew gave me worried look. I reassured him everything would be fine and told him to take his pen and paper and book to his room.

Mr. Catron entered and greeted me cordially, though his countenance was grim. This did not bode well. I was certain Charles had sent instructions to pack Matthew's things and send him off to Philadelphia or Boston or some such place, the further away the better, in Charles's mind.

We sat down. A cool breeze wafted through the open windows. The sheer green curtains billowed gently.

Mrs. Medrano brought in a pitcher of water and two glasses on a tray, set them down on the table then left.

"I received this telegram and came directly over," he said, taking the folded yellow paper from his valise. He held it out to me, and I asked him if he wouldn't mind telling me what it said. It may sound petty, but truthfully, I did not want to touch it.

202

Mr. Catron cleared his throat but did not look at the telegram. "Charles is dead," he said.

I could not believe it. Were my ears playing tricks on me?

"It happened last evening," Mr. Catron went on. "Charles was shot by a ruffian." He cleared his throat again. "A young woman Charles was escorting to supper, a Miss Evelyn Hobbs, was wearing a pearl necklace and the robber put his hands on her in an attempt to steal it. She slapped the assailant and the pistol he was holding fired. The bullet struck Charles in the back."

I leaned forward in my chair. "Did you say in the back?"

"Yes," he said. "He was," he cleared his throat again, "running. Perhaps to fetch help. At least that is what the police believe. Miss Hobbs screamed, and the assailant dropped his pistol and ran as well."

Stunned I was. Charles Preston, the snobby gentleman toad, was also a cowardly toad.

"And who was this woman?" I asked.

"May I trouble you for a glass of water?" Mr. Catron asked.

I held the pitcher and filled a glass. He took it from me gratefully and nearly drained it. I filled it again.

He thanked me and continued. "Charles was in negotiations with several clients in Denver regarding business opportunities they wished to explore here in New Mexico Territory. He traveled to Denver on a number of occasions." He took another drink of water. "During this time, it appears that he made the acquaintance of Miss Hobbs, a wealthy and influential scion of Denver society, and took a regrettably keen interest in her."

"How long?"

"Pardon me?"

"How long had he been seeing her?"

"From what I can gather, almost from the beginning. About two years."

My Father told Brigid and I that we must try to live by the Ten Commandments, for if we did not, we have no chance to attain the promise of heaven. I hoped Charles was screaming in the fires of hell.

"You have my deepest sympathies, Miss Danaher," Mr. Catron said.

I thanked him.

"Now then," he said, "I don't wish to appear indelicate but, given these extraordinary circumstances, I thought it best to make you aware of the provisions of Charles's last will and testament, if I may."

"It would probably be best to know, for the sake of the children."

"Precisely." He pulled several papers from his valise. "I read his will over before coming here. The children will inherit everything. Of course, they are far too young to take on that kind of responsibility. That leaves us in a prickly situation. Charles had no other living relative. So, as Brigid's sister, the responsibility falls to you."

Mother once said that orphans would be my children and my happiness. Matthew and Anne needed me more than ever now. And, the truth be told, I needed them.

"I took the liberty of consulting with Judge Longwell before coming over," Mr. Catron said. "He concurs with me that, with your approval, a proposal I have might be the best solution."

"Please go on."

He said he and I would act in concert. He would take the duties of the executor, overseeing the expenses and the care of the estate, and I would become the legal guardian of the children, seeing to their welfare, until they became of age to take over the responsibilities of the estate and its holdings.

"Charles's holdings are considerable," he said. "About a million and a half dollars, between cash and properties."

"My Lord."

"And, of course, I shall take over all of Charles's pending cases. Any and all monies earned will be deposited into the estate for the benefit of the children. Charles was quite skilled as an attorney. Almost as adept as myself, I assure you." He slipped the will back inside his valise. "As for young Mathew's predicament, allow me to speak with Brother Butolph. I've been known to be quite persuasive."

I thanked him for that.

"I'll start preparing the legal documents," he said. "Meanwhile, I am at your disposal to discuss any concerns you might have."

I told him I understood.

After showing him out, I turned, and Mrs. Medrano came into the foyer. I told her everything.

Her eyes welled with tears. "This will be so difficult for the children," she said. "When should we tell them?"

"Not today," I said gently.

She stared at me.

I said, "We're taking them to the celebration this evening. I do not wish to spoil that for them. Tomorrow is Saturday. That will be soon enough."

"But he is their father."

"Charles wanted nothing to do with them until he decided they were worthy of his time. They have been burdened enough with his pettiness and uncaring ways. Tomorrow will be fine."

"Forgive me," she said, "but I still do not think that is right."

"Perhaps not. But I believe it's the decent thing, the best thing, for Mathew and Anne."

"*Sí, senorita.*"

I could see from her expression she was not happy with my decision. But it was my decision.

I hoped Brigid was not upset with me.

# Chapter Thirty-Six

"Did Father send word where I would be sent away to school?" Matthew asked when I entered his room. He was standing with his back to the door, looking out of the window. He did not turn around.

"No, he did not."

"What did Mr. Catron want then?"

"Nothing to concern yourself with."

Matthew raised his hand and waved at something outside.

"Who's out there?" I asked.

"The sister. She's down there, by the river."

Just as I joined him at the window he said, "She's gone."

"A sister, you said."

He nodded. "She was walking down the road heading for the river."

That road separated our property from the archbishop's.

"How do you know it was a sister you saw?" I asked.

"She was dressed in black."

"Have you seen her before?"

"Yesterday."

I wondered if it was the one from Anne's school I had accosted by the bridge.

"She waves to me when she sees me," he said.

"When was that?"

"Yesterday afternoon. This is the second time she's passed by today."

I stood closer to the window to try to see over by the river. Could it be that black wretch he saw? No. Impossible. It had to have been the sister, just as he said.

"Let's go back downstairs and continue the lesson," I said. "Get your book then."

As he started out the door, I could not help looking out the window again. I saw no figure in black walking by. But an uncomfortable feeling overcame me. It was as though I was being watched.

Downstairs, I found Mr. Jessup waiting for me.

"I just need a moment, ma'am," he said.

I told Matthew to go on into the sitting room.

"I wanted to ask what time you would like to leave for the celebration tonight," Mr. Jessup said.

"What have you done before?"

"Mrs. Preston liked to leave about an hour before dark. She said that gave Matthew and Anne time to look around a little bit and then we'd get a good spot on San Francisco Street to watch the procession."

"That sounds splendid," I said.

"It's a full moon tonight."

"That will be nice."

"But I believe it's going to turn colder," he went on. "I'll light the fireplaces before we leave. Come home to a warm house."

"That's very considerate." I motioned to him to follow me. Passing the tower sitting room, I told Matthew I'd return in a moment. Mr. Jessup and I went outside onto the front porch.

"Now," I said, keeping my voice low, "you should know that Mr. Catron came by this morning with news."

"Mrs. Medrano already told me, ma'am. About Mr. Preston."

"That's fine then. But I don't want you to say anything about it to the children. I'll tell them tomorrow."

"That's wise," he said. "Any help I can be, let me know."

I told him I appreciated that, but I sensed there was something else on his mind.

"Ma'am, if you don't mind my saying, Mrs. Medrano also told me about telling you, well, about her son."

"Oh?"

"Don't take it wrong, ma'am. We're not talking about you behind your back. She fixes me coffee every morning and we talk a little bit. The point is, she told me on account of she said she's worried."

"About what?"

"About you and this crying woman and hearing voices and all. She's afraid for you and says you ought to be scared. But I told her. From what I've seen, you aren't scared of anything. You got gumption, ma'am. More than most in my opinion."

# Chapter Thirty-Seven

**M**rs. Medrano was quiet during the afternoon meal. She hardly looked at me. Undoubtedly my decision about not telling the children about their Father still rankled her. I did not believe Matthew noticed, at least not that I could see.

After my mid-afternoon prayers, I went downstairs, unsure of my destination. The house was quiet. In his room, Matthew read *David Copperfield*. Mrs. Medrano prepared supper out in the kitchen.

Something drew me to the dancing parlor. Inside I found the burgundy-colored drapes and curtains were pulled open. The three Persian rugs lay neatly on the wooden floor. The black piano sat silent at the opposite end of the parlor. And over the great marble fireplace hung Brigid's portrait, her face angelic and her eyes filled with melancholy. I stepped closer.

"I wish you were here with me," I whispered. "I love you and I miss you so. There's much I want to talk to you about. Things have changed yet again, and I hope I'm making the right choices, for the sake of the children. I want to do the best for them. To raise them the way you would have done. Please, help me, Brigid." I started for the door and turned back to her portrait. "And let me know if I'm doing wrong."

# Chapter Thirty-Eight

ater that day, Mr. Jessup brought Anne home from school. She came skipping up the front steps humming a pleasant tune. It had a singsong quality, like a nursery rhyme. Something she must have learned in school, I decided. I told her we would be leaving for the celebration tonight soon after supper. She smiled; her eyes brightened.

I was pleased at the excitement the children expressed during the meal. They recalled the wonderful time they had had at the festivities the previous year. Even Mrs. Medrano had softened her frown, smiling at me, and saying it would be a good night for all of us.

We finished supper and I told the children to go to their rooms and wash their faces and change their clothes. I went to my room to pray the Divine Office. It wasn't long before Anne came knocking at my door needing help with the dress and pinafore she'd chosen to wear. I set aside my book of prayers. I would finish my reading later, after we came home. The last lines I read were from the gospel of John. *Do not let your heart be troubled. You have faith in God.*

As I buttoned up her dress, Anne began humming her tune from earlier. I told her I thought it was pretty and asked what it was.

"I don't know," she said.

"Did you hear it at school then?"

"No. It was when Mr. Jessup was bringing me home."

"Some children were singing it, were they?"

"I think it was only one girl."

"How do you know?"

"That was all I heard. I couldn't see who she was. I guess she was playing under the bridge."

A disquieting feeling came over me. "A little girl under the bridge?"

"It sounded like a girl. Do you want to hear the words?"

"Oh, there are words. Yes, I would."

She sang them softly. "Come to me children. Come to the riverside. Come to me children. Do not try to hide."

A shiver spiraled up my back and the hairs on the back of my neck stood out.

"That's nice, sweetheart," I said as I slipped the pinafore over her head and straightened it out. "Get your coat and let's go downstairs then. I need to see Mr. Jessup."

I found him outside by the surrey adjusting the straps on the horses.

He saw me coming and said, "Not to worry, ma'am. I'll light all the fireplaces before we leave. The rooms will be good and warm when we return."

"Of course, Mr. Jessup," I said, trying to keep the urgency out of my voice, "but I need to ask you a question. Did you happen to hear singing when you brought Anne home today?"

"Yes, ma'am. Twice."

"Twice?"

"Taking her to school and again coming back."

"You didn't mention it before."

"I didn't see the reason. It was only some girl sitting by the river."

"You mean you saw her?"

He nodded. "Just sitting there. Not much bigger than Matthew, I'd say."

"How was she dressed?"

He frowned. "I don't recall exactly."

"Anything, Mr. Jessup."

"I'm sorry, ma'am. She had her head down and her hair covered her face. I believe her hair was black, though."

I thanked him and started back to the house.

"It's a pretty song, don't you think?" he called after me. "Anne took right to it."

A feeling of dread would not leave me this day. As much as I tried, I could not dispel it. First that terrible nightmare, then Charles, and then Matthew waving to a dark figure, and now Anne and that song. Was there any truth to this Weeping Woman curse? Even as I had said my daily prayers, something sinister taunted me.

I carried that trepidation with me as we rode to town and tried my best not to reveal it to the others.

We walked along San Francisco Avenue with its bonfires of *piñon* wood already ablaze, throwing shimmering firelight across the *adobe* storefronts stretching from the cathedral to the *plaza*. More small fires burned along the the streets surrounding the *plaza*. And there, in the center of the town, to the delight of the children, the Chinese lanterns glowed, suspended from the lines strung between the trees the workmen had been hanging earlier.

The town fire department volunteers stood on the corner in front of the Exchange Hotel. Close by was their horse-drawn red wagon with a fire hose rolled onto a wooden reel and a large canister of water sitting up in the bed, ready in the event any errant cinders started a fire.

Mr. Spiegelberg stood outside his store with his wife, a cheerful woman with her hair piled up on top of her head. In their hands they held large trays arrayed with cookies, offering them to passers-by. The cookies were *biscochitos*, the same kind that Doctor Symington's wife had served me the other day.

"Take two," Mrs. Spiegelberg told Matthew and Anne. "One for each hand."

We crossed the street to the *plaza* to take a closer look at the Chinese lanterns.

"Aunt Catherine?" Anne asked.

"Yes?"

"Are you having a nice time?"

"Of course, I am, sweetheart. Why do you ask?"

"You don't look very happy."

"I'm enjoying myself as much as you are," I said. Lord help me, did I appear so anxious that even a child could see it?

Shortly, a procession of marchers gathered on the *plaza*, bundled against the crisp evening air, and began the walk up the street toward the cathedral. Each carried a lighted candle and sang a hymn. Near the front of the procession was the archbishop, dressed in his white vestments, singing, and smiling. As he passed by, he saw us and nodded. I noticed the edge of a woolen scarf peeking up from under the neck of his vestments. On reaching the great front doors of the cathedral, the procession turned and concluded their singing.

The archbishop spoke. "I welcome you to this feast of St. Francis of Assisi, the patron saint of—"

His voice, strong at first, suddenly failed, likely due to his cold.

I couldn't hear any more of what he said, but he spoke very briefly and then the fireworks shot into the air from old Fort Marcy then burst in the sky. A grand illumination it was. Music played. In front of the cathedral, the St. Francis band had assembled with their trumpets, tubas, and drums. The children beamed with delight.

The time came to return home. And for reasons I could not explain that grim, dreadful feeling had thankfully passed.

# Chapter Thirty-Nine

The sounds of the celebration around the *plaza* grew fainter as we drove along Palace Avenue, our way lit by both the moon and the lanterns on either side of the surrey.

We covered our legs with blankets Mr. Jessup kept under the seats of the surrey. I thanked him for his thoughtfulness.

Matthew and Anne and Mrs. Medrano talked of how wonderful the evening had been. Anne sat between Mrs. Medrano and me while Mr. Jessup made room on his seat for Matthew.

I looked up and saw the moon, bright and white in the black sky sprinkled with thousands of twinkling stars. God's own firmament.

We turned onto the long driveway. Bathed in the moonlight, the house seemed almost inviting. Through a couple of the windows, I could see the yellow glow of fireplaces burning.

Drawing closer, I heard something. A small voice, singing soft and low. "Come to me children. Do not try to hide." I glanced down at Anne. Her head was resting against my shoulder.

"Anne?" I whispered.

She tilted her head up at me.

"Was that you singing just now?" I asked.

"No," she said. "I thought it was you."

Oh, Lord, was I hearing things again?

"Here we are," Mr. Jessup said, reining to a stop by the front porch.

Matthew jumped from his seat. I climbed down and lifted Anne from the surrey while Mrs. Medrano got out on the opposite side.

"Ma'am?" I heard Mr. Jessup say. "If you have no objection, I'd like to—"

The horses squealed and reared, legs pawing frantically at the dark. The surrey shook. Mr. Jessup tried to control the team. Something swooped by me and struck Mr. Jessup. He fell, hitting the ground hard. The horses reared again.

Anne screamed. I pulled her away.

Mrs. Medrano took hold of a loose rein. "Mr. Jessup!" she cried, moving around in front of the horses.

Matthew tried to help her.

A horrible wailing cry rose up.

"No, no, no!" Mrs. Medrano shouted. "It is her! *¡Santa María, Madre de Dios! ¡Santa María, Madre de Dios!*"

The horses snorted, reared again, jerking the rein from Mrs. Medrano's hands. She tumbled backwards, knocking Matthew down. The horses bolted, pulling the surrey over Mr. Jessup's unmoving body.

I pushed Anne toward the house. "Run children! Get to the house!"

Matthew got to his feet, snatched his sister's hand, and pulled her up the stairs.

Mrs. Medrano was dragging Mr. Jessup to the house. "*Santa María, Madre de Dios. Santa María, Madre de Dios.*"

The wailing was all around us now. Where was it coming from? Coldness descended. A black shape whirled past Mrs. Medrano and threw her to the ground.

God, please, it can't be. I got to her side. Blood covered her face.

The terrible wail became howling words. "*¿Dónde están mis hijos?*"

Mrs. Medrano clutched my arm. "*La Llorona.* It is *La Llorona!*"

"Bring me my children!"

Inside the house Anne screamed.

"She's after the children!" Mrs. Medrano whimpered.

Up the stairs I ran, two at a time. Anne stood in the foyer, her body shaking. She had wet herself, a puddle at her feet.

"Get out!" Matthew cried. "Get out!" He was in Charles's library. I told Anne to go to Mrs. Medrano then I rushed inside. My eyes grew wide in horror. A floating black specter in a tattered dress and veil loomed before Matthew, cackling and taunting him. Matthew held a burning piece of firewood from the fireplace in both his hands, swinging it wildly. Bright cinders flew and orange flames singed the air.

"Get back!" he shouted, moving in closer to it.

Cackling louder, the specter drew back toward the curtained window.

"Matthew! No!" I shouted.

An evil hiss filled the room. The specter turned toward me. Through its ragged black veil, I saw its face. A beautiful woman it was. Almost angelic. Her inviting smile turned vicious as her face dissolved into a coarse old crone. She opened her mouth wide. Out came that awful wail.

Matthew lunged. The specter swirled away, and Matthew's flame struck the curtains and they caught fire instantly.

Startled, Matthew dropped the burning wood.

Flames leapt from curtains to bookshelves.

The specter wailed and began to spin, her tattered robes fanning the flames. Burning shards of paper whirled into the air. The fireplace flames burst forth, like a fiery hand reaching out. The velvet covered chairs and wooden tables caught fire. Flames consumed Charles's desk. Thick smoke curled around us. I pulled Matthew out of the room.

In the foyer, Anne still stood, scared and shaking.

"Take your sister and get out of the house," I told Matthew. "Find Mrs. Medrano!"

I looked back. Smoke and flame licked up the walls of the foyer, reaching the second landing. God help us.

Outside, Anne screamed.

"Let go!" Matthew shouted. "Let us go!"

That thing had them!

I ran outside and down the front porch stairs. The children's screams came from around the side of the house. My God, it was taking them to the river!

"Catherine hurry!" Mrs. Medrano cried out. "Help them!"

Bundling the front of my skirt in my fist, I chased after my children.

The specter had each of them by an arm, dragging them across the garden. The blackness of the thing possessed a sheen in the moonlight, like a raven's feathers.

I ran past the house and into the garden.

"Come with me children! Come and play!" The thing cackled. It had reached the trellis. With his one free hand, Matthew took hold of the edge of a bench there. "Help! Help!" he cried.

The thing pulled at him. Matthew held fast. The thing floated up off the ground and jerked him loose. Anne dangled limply from the thing's black arm.

"No!" Matthew screamed as it lifted him into the air.

God help me, please! I ran straight for them. Rose bush thorns cut into my legs. I leapt over thick shrubs. Tall yellow flowers scratched at my arms.

The thing reached the line of young fruit trees. It was nearly to the river!

I ran past the trellis and saw Matthew still fighting to free himself from the grip of the thing. My foot went out from under me. I slid into a rose bed. Thorns stuck my legs, arms, face. I didn't care. Pulling myself free, my dress tore. I stumbled, kept running, my heart thumping in my chest.

The thing had disappeared! And the children. Where were they? The river!

"Matthew! Anne!" I shouted, reaching the ugly, dead tree. "Matthew! Where are you? Anne!"

Oh God, I was too late. No! Please! I looked up and down the river, praying for a sign. There was only the gentle sound of the flowing waters.

"Anne! Answer me!"

Splashing. I saw Anne's head appear above the water. I jumped into the river. Lord it was cold. I'm coming, sweetheart. Her head went under, her arms flailing. I reached out, caught one of her tiny hands in mine. Something powerful pulled both of us under the water. Keeping my eyes open, I saw the black thing held her fast, but I did not see Matthew. I refused to let go of Anne. I needed air. My feet found purchase on the bedrock. My face cleared the surface. Anne's hand was still in mine. Drawing breath, I went back under. The thing was gone. Anne's body floated there at the end of my arm. No! I pulled her up. Please, God. Breathe, Anne. Breathe. She coughed up water as I lifted her onto the embankment. Thank you, Lord.

"Matthew," she cried weakly.

"I'll find him."

I called his name, praying for his deliverance. My feet were bare. I had lost my shoes in the river. I felt for my Mother's crucifix. It was still around my neck. My woolen dress lay wet and heavy on me.

"Help me!" It was Matthew. I ran to him. The thing had him. He was halfway out of the water, crawling up the embankment, hands reaching out. The thing was dragging him back down into the water. I took hold of his arm. Anne cried out my name. The smell of rotting flesh surrounded me. Something gripped my shoulder and forced me to the ground. A grotesque hand reached out for Matthew. The thing's hellish voice filled my ears, "My children!"

"No!" I shouted.

The thing turned on me, its face now withered and worm-eaten. "They are mine!" it wailed then lunged at Matthew and they disappeared beneath the water.

Scrambling to my feet, I plunged in after them.

The black thing swirled under the water before me. I clawed at it but could not take a hold. It seethed and roiled, as though angered at my presence. Something kicked by me. Matthew! Had the thing let him go? My head broke the surface. I drew sweet breath. Matthew crawled up the embankment.

I reached out to grasp the riverbank. I felt so cold, my dress like a weight. The black specter flew out of the river before me, water, glistening like rivulets of silver, ran down its blackness. It wailed its awful cry, took me by the throat, and dragged me under the water.

Something sharp snagged my dress. A broken branch held me fast to that spot.

The specter's grip tightened around my throat. I tried to break its hold with my hands, but the blackness dissolved between my fingers then somehow condensed again. It was like sinking my hands into murky silt. My fingers went numb.

Shimmering light shone from above. I saw fire then faces through the water. Men with torches ran along the embankment searching. I heard their muffled shouts. "She's in there!" "Find her!" I wanted to cry out, I'm here! Help me! My lungs screamed for air. Instinct made me draw a breath, but water flooded my mouth then into my lungs.

221

I clawed for the surface, for that precious air. But the thing held me down. Something twisted tight around my neck. The chain of my crucifix! The fiend was trying to choke me with it! My lungs ached. My eyes squeezed shut. Please, Lord, save me! I don't want to die! Don't want... Save the children... Must save...

I felt my soul slipping away.

And the thing spoke, its vile mouth by my ear. "Your sister came to the river that night. She wanted to cut down my tree."

A scene appeared before my eyes. Moonlight shone on the river. Brigid looking up at the tree, an angry look on her face, shaking her head.

The thing spoke. "I drowned her."

I saw Brigid's terrified face through the moonlit waters, her mouth open in a silent scream, her eyes closing.

"You heard my cries," the thing said. "Now I drown you. And then those cursed children of yours!"

Something had changed about me. A fire rose in my belly. This evil had murdered Brigid. It would not harm the children. Strength Lord! Renew my strength! I felt my fingers sink into the thing, taking firm hold now! I pried one of its hands free. The eyes of the horrid thing widened in surprise. It struggled against my grasp and twisted the chain tighter about my neck. I closed my hands around the throat of this devil. The Lord was helping me to save the children from this horror!

The specter thrashed about.

God, please, help me fight!

Water churned. Blackness swirled.

My crucifix chain drew tighter around my neck, digging deeper into my skin.

"This won't protect you," the thing cried.

I held fast to the specter with a holy fervor. God was answering my prayer! Do not let me fail!

A loud pealing resounded. A heavenly sound it was. Was it the San Miguel chapel bell? Could it be? But how? That bell lay on the ground.

The thing threw its head back, screaming like a banshee, a horrible painful wail, too awful to describe. Like the cry Mrs. Medrano said her son had heard. The blackness vanished before my eyes. I felt myself floating. As light as the ether, I was.

The river current pushed me to the embankment. I lay there, half in the water. The men carrying torches had not yet seen me. I reached for my Mother's crucifix. It and the chain were gone! No! I raised my head, peering about, looking for it. Had the thing torn it from around my neck?

"Don't tell me you didn't hear that!" one of the men shouted.

"I heard it, clear as anything."

"I'm telling you; it was the bell at San Miguel chapel."

I smiled. The legend was true after all.

Through the trees, I saw a fiery glow in the sky. The house had become an inferno. The firemen raced up in their horse-drawn wagon. Manning the canister pump handles, they worked vigorously and had a good stream of water from the hose arching into the flames. People formed a line with buckets of water. But the children! Were they safe? I saw them. Mrs. Medrano held them close to her. Blankets wrapped around them. Anne's face was buried in the folds of Mrs. Medrano's skirt.

Men were coming. I heard their footfalls approaching and saw the torches.

"Find her!" one shouted.

I pulled myself up, still looking for my Mother's crucifix. I had to find it. Where was it?

"Here she is!" a fellow in a derby hat cried.

More came running.

"Look there! What's that?" another said, standing some yards back up near the edge of the river. He held a torch in his hand.

"What do you see?" a tall man said, and I saw the badge pinned to his chest.

"In the rocks there. See it glinting in the light?"

Bringing his torch closer to the ground, the deputy reached down and picked something up. The crucifix and chain of my Mother hung from his fingers.

"Must be the lady's," the deputy said.

My hand flew to my mouth. Thank you, Lord. It was not lost. Anne would wear it around her neck one day. My orphans were safe. Evil beaten.

# Chapter Forty

The archbishop said Charles's funeral Mass. Charles was buried next to Brigid at Rosario Cemetery. It was only proper, I suppose. Matthew and Anne laid flowers from Brigid's garden on his grave. They looked so very sad. Many people came and paid their respects, Mr. Catron, Doctor Symington, and Mr. Spiegelberg among them. I overheard them saying they had come for the sake of the children. They never mentioned Charles by name.

The fire had nearly consumed the house. The decision was made not to rebuild it. For one, the children did not want to live in it. Too many bad memories, they said. Mr. Catron agreed. Rebuilding the house, he said, would present an unfortunate reminder to everyone of the sad and deplorable life Charles had led. Mr. Catron purchased the property, for more than it was worth, I might add, and eventually sold it as housing lots. Half of those proceeds he placed in the trust he established for the children.

Sadly, Brigid's garden did not survive as she had hoped it would. The following month, a terrible storm caused the river to overflow, destroying most of it.

We lived in a small house Mr. Catron happened to own in town rent-free while a new house, smaller and less ostentatious than Charles's mansion, was built on a lot further up on Palace Avenue.

Mr. Catron owned that lot, as well, but sold it to the estate for the sum of one dollar.

During Mr. Catron's handling of the administrative chores of Charles's estate, there was never so much as a penny unaccounted for. In spite of troubles that plagued Mr. Catron—accusations of dishonest dealings, bribery, and various other scandals—he dealt properly with the estate, as well as seeing to the children's welfare and their future as if they were his own.

I was also very pleased that Mr. Catron had the dead tree by the river cut down and burned. The curse of *La Llorona* never befell him or his family. Perhaps she was afraid of him.

I continued my duties of caring for Matthew and Anne. Helping them prepare their lessons, brushing away their tears when they cried, laughing with them when they were happy. I saw to protecting them. *La Llorona* never again tried to snatch them up or lure them to the river. Matthew and Anne were mine. The Weeping Woman knew better than to try to clash with me again. I had bested her, even without that bell ringing and scaring her away. I believe she was afraid of me now, too. She should be.

Mrs. Medrano remained as both housekeeper and cook. Mr. Jessup also stayed on with his duties and surprised us all when he announced that he and Mrs. Medrano were getting married. A grand wedding it was, too, held in the cathedral. Archbishop Lamy performed the ceremony. The flowers were from his garden. Did I mention that Mr. Jessup became a Catholic? Mrs. Medrano had insisted.

God called the good archbishop home five years later. People traveled hundreds of miles to attend his funeral. Sadly, he did not live long enough to see his dream, his cathedral, completed, plagued as he was by a persistent lack of money. Many people, I found out, called the cathedral Lamy's folly. Shame on them, I thought. Of course, Mr.

Jessup said, as only Mr. Jessup could, that if God ever thought He had a foolish idea, He could ask the archbishop for counsel because the archbishop was the master of foolish ideas.

Doctor Symington set Matthew's broken arm a few years later when Matthew fell out of a tree. He also sewed a new leg on Anne's doll when she brought it to him for mending following an unfortunate incident involving a meat cleaver.

After living here for many years, Mr. Spiegelberg, his wife and their two daughters left Santa Fe in the summer of 1888. He had decided to follow his brothers and move to New York City. People said the store wasn't the same without them there.

The following summer, Sheriff Martínez was appointed a United States Marshal for the Territory of New Mexico. Of the stories that circulated about him, the one I liked best happened during a Christmas celebration at the cathedral. A man brazenly stole money from the poor box. Marshal Martínez, dressed as one of the three wise men, was not wearing his revolver. With his long robes billowing and a gold crown on his head, he pursued the miscreant down San Francisco Street, apprehending the scoundrel after he walloped him with his bag of myrrh.

Since Matthew enjoyed the dime novels written by Mr. Fairchild, I always kept a keen eye out for them, but Mr. Fairchild never penned another, at least that I saw. However, I did hear a rumor that he had gone to California and was soon elected to the state legislature there.

Whether it was the intercession of Archbishop Lamy or Mr. Catron I never found out, but Brother Butolph did allow Matthew to return to St. Michael's. In return, Matthew promised to work very hard. He kept that promise and later became a writer of some renown, documenting not only the history of New Mexico, but also writing acclaimed novels of the West, inspired, in part, by those dime novels he had enjoyed as a child. I am pleased that he somehow took the luridness of those dime novels and spun them into lyrical stories of courage and honor.

A few years after graduating from Loretto Academy, Anne married a kind and decent man; a lawyer who was elected to the territorial legislature and later became governor. Anne never let him forget he was responsible to the people.

Matthew also married. His wife had come west with her family from Pittsburgh of all places. They had lived three houses down from where Mother and Father and Brigid and I had lived.

Both Matthew and Anne had children of their own, and I watched over them, as well. And when their children were of age to understand, they brought them to Rosario Cemetery, and Matthew and Anne placed fresh flowers on my grave.

"We only knew Aunt Catherine for a few days," Matthew said. "But she cared about us very much. She drowned in the river saving our lives that terrible night years ago."

Anne touched the silver crucifix hanging from a delicate chain around her neck that had been my Mother's and said, "I do think she's been watching over us ever since."

I always knew I would never have children of my own. Mother said the orphans would be my children, my happiness.

# *Author's Note*

I am deeply grateful to my friends who willingly shared their stories about growing up in Santa Fe, New Mexico, and their experiences regarding *La Llorona*, the Weeping Woman.

They told me that when they were children, their parents warned them to beware of her. One said he first heard about *La Llorona* from his mother just before going out on Halloween night. She told him to stay away from the river or *La Llorona* would catch him. Another recalled when she was a little girl, she was awakened late one night by the most horrible of cries coming from the Santa Fe River. "I've never heard anything else like it," she said. "It scared me to death." Still another story went that one sunny afternoon, two young girlfriends walking home from the movies saw a tall figure dressed in a hooded black robe coming at them from down the street. Terrified, they ran inside a store, looked out the window and saw the figure had vanished. One of the girls called home and begged her father to come pick them up. "My dad asked where we were. I told him. He said, 'But you're only a block from home.' I said, 'Please, come get us.' We were so scared."

According to noted Santa Fe storyteller and cultural historian Nasario Garcia, the legend of *La Llorona* came to the Americas when the Spanish conquistadores landed here in the 16th Century. One of the earliest stories concerns Marina La Malinche, a woman of the

Nahua, an indigenous people of Mexico, who acted as interpreter for Hernán Cortés, who led the Spanish conquest of the Aztec Empire. The story goes that she became Cortés' mistress and bore him children, but rather than see them raised as Spaniards, she murdered them.

Another version tells of a commoner woman who married a nobleman. Later, he deserted her and their two children. Tormented, she killed her children with a knife and was burned at the stake as a witch.

Then there is the story of Maria, a beautiful but vain village girl who refused the advances of local boys as she has set her eyes on the son of a wealthy landowner. One day he noticed her, and they soon married. Maria bore him two children and soon afterward, her husband lost interest in her, finding comfort in the arms of other younger women. Seeing him in town with one his new women, Maria dragged her children to the river, drowned them and then killed herself. Her spirit now walks and wails through the night near rivers or streams or arroyos, calling out for her dead children.

Still other variations of the *La Llorona* myth exist. One says she was a good woman who seeks forgiveness for her terrible act; while another goes that she fell in love with a rich grandee and became pregnant. He refused to marry her and when she gave birth to her child, she drowned it in the river to hide her shame. Some believe her apparition snatches only children, while others say she attacks any man, woman or child who is foolish enough to come to the river. She is also said to lure cheating spouses to the river and drown them. And still others have claimed she appeared to them when they were children, delivering warnings to obey their parents or she would visit them again.

Descriptions of *La Llorona* vary, as well. Her face has been described as alluring and framed with long flowing black hair. It is also said she has the contorted features of an old hag, a skull-like face, or the head of a horse. While some are certain she is dressed in white, others are positive they have seen her draped in black.

In Santa Fe, New Mexico, it is said she haunts not only the Santa Fe River, but also a New Mexico State Government building located not far from the river called the PERA Building (the Public Employees Retirement Association), which was built on land that was an old graveyard.

*La Llorona* has been seen and heard in New Mexico, Arizona, California, Colorado, Oklahoma, Kansas, Texas, Wyoming, and as far north as Montana and North Dakota. Other sightings have been reported in Mexico, El Salvador, Honduras, Guatemala, Panama, and even Chile.

It is a legend that continues to be passed from mothers to daughters and fathers to sons. Is there any truth to the story? Who knows? But there are those who are absolutely certain *La Llorona* is real. The reason, they say, is because they cannot forget what they saw and heard.

As to my novel, it is a work of fiction, but Thomas B. Catron, Doctor John Symington, Sheriff Frank (Francisco) Martínez, Archbishop Jean-Baptiste Lamy, and Brother Butolph are not inventions. They all lived in Santa Fe at the time my story takes place. However, their words are mine.

Also, in my story, the Spanish words that *La Llorona* speaks are those that have been reported over the centuries, however, her English words are mine. And while I have neither seen nor heard *La Llorona* myself, I could not resist the idea of her for this tale I've told.

In Santa Fe, New Mexico, I wish to thank Frank Romero, Curator, San Miguel Mission Church, and David Blackman with the Preserve San Miguel organization for their invaluable information about the

San Miguel Mission Church. They graciously answered my questions and offered their own stories.

The history of the city of Santa Fe proved an experience fraught with difficulties and contradictions. I am indebted to a number of individuals who helped me sort things out. At the New Mexico State Library, Southwest Collection, my sincere thanks and appreciation to Laura Calderone, Reference Service Manager, Lori Thornton, Public Services Bureau Chief, and Faith Yoman, Southwest Librarian, for their expertise and patience.

Also, many thanks to Patricia Hewitt, Senior Cataloguer, the Fray Angelico Chavez History Library, and to Emily Ray Brock and Hanna Abelbeck, Photo Archivists, at the New Mexico History Museum, Palace of the Governors, Photo Archives. Their assistance proved most rewarding.

For information about *La Llorona* I consulted *Cuentos from My Childhood: Legends and Folktales of Northern New Mexico* by Paulette Atencio, Museum of New Mexico Press, 1991; *Brujerias, Stories of Witchcraft and the Supernatural in the American Southwest and Beyond* by Nasario García, Texas Tech University Press, 2007; *Grandma's Santo on Its Head/El santo pata arriba de mi abuelita* by Nasario García, University of New Mexico Press, 2013; *Handbook of Hispanic Culture in the United States: Literature and Art*, edited by Nicolás Kanellos and Claudio Estava-Fabregat, Arte Público Press, 1993; and the online article, "The Legend of La Llorona, the Ghost of the Rio Grande" by Paul Harden, *El Defensor Chieftain*, December 1, 2007 (www.elcaminoreal.org/PH/1207_llorona.pdf ).

There are scores of books about the history of old Santa Fe and New Mexico. The sources I used were *Desert Lawmen: The High Sheriffs of New Mexico and Arizona, 1846-1912* by Larry D. Ball, University of New Mexico Press, 2011; *Light in Yucca Land; 1852-1952* by Sister

Richard Marie Barbour, Loretto Academy of Our Lady of Light, 1952; *Santa Fe Tales & More* by Howard Bryan, Clear Light Publishers, 2010; *Chasing the Santa Fe Ring, Power and Privilege in Territorial New Mexico* by David L. Caffey, University of New Mexico Press, 2014; *Deadly Dozen: Twelve Forgotten Gunfighters of the Old West, Volume 1* by Robert K. DeArment, University of Oklahoma Press, 2015; *Letters from the Southwest, September 20, 1884 to March 14, 1885* by Charles Fletcher Lummis, University of Arizona Press, 1989; *The Social History of the United States: The 1900s* by Brian Greenberg and Linda S. Watts, ABC-CLIO, Inc, 2009; *Germans in the Southwest, 1850-1920* by Tomas Jaehn, University of New Mexico Press, 2005; *The Real Roadrunner* by Martha Anne Maxon, University of Oklahoma Press, 2005; *Buried Treasures: Famous and Unusual Gravesites in New Mexico History* by Richard Melzer, Sunstone Press, 2007; *Frontiers of Femininity: A New Historical Geography of the Nineteenth-Century American West* by Karen Morin, Syracuse University Press, 2008; *Black-Robed Justice* by Arie W. Poldervaart, Historical Society of New Mexico, 1948; *Spanish Mission Churches of New Mexico* by L. Bradford Prince, The Torch Press, 1915; *Santa Fe: A Pictorial History* by John Sherman, The Donning Company, 1996; *Santa Fe: A Modern History, 1880-1990* by Henry J. Tobias and Charles E. Woodhouse, University of New Mexico Press, 2001; *The Land of the Pueblos* by Susan Elston Wallace, John B. Alden, Publisher, 1888. Articles I consulted were "Militia Posses: The Territorial Militia in Civil Law Enforcement in New Mexico Territory, 1877-1883" by Larry D. Ball, *New Mexico Historical Review*, Vol. 55, No. 1, January 1980; "The Hayt-Wientge Mansion" by James H. Purdy, *The Historic Santa Fe Foundation Bulletin*, Vol. 2, No.1, Spring-Summer 1976; "The Willi Spiegelberg House" by James H. Purdy, *The Historic Santa Fe Foundation Bulletin*, Vol. 4, No. 1, May/June 1978; and "Flora Spiegelberg," (www.storiesuntold.

org/women/flora_test.html).

For material on the Sisters of Mercy I read *Memoirs of the Pittsburgh Sisters of Mercy, Compiled From Various Sources, 1843-1917*, The Devin-Adair Company, 1918.

For background on the Christian Brothers I went to *A Hundred Years of Service: St. Michael's High School Centennial 1859-1959*, The Brothers of the Christian School, 1959; *75 Years of Service 1859-1934: An Historical Sketch of Saint Michael's College*, St. Michael's College, 1934; *The Catholic World*, Volume 79, Published by the Paulist Fathers, Office of the Catholic World, 1901; *To Touch Hearts – Pedagogical Spirituality and St. John Baptist de La Salle*, a dissertation by George Van Grieken, FSC, Boston College, 2011; and the article "Communal Prayer in the 1718 and 1987 Editions of the Rule of the Brothers of the Christian Schools" by Peter Killeen, FSC, *AXIS: Journal of Lasallian Higher Education* 3, no. 3, (Institute for Lasallian Studies at Saint Mary's University of Minnesota: 2012).

For insight on Irish legends and folklore I consulted *The Dead-watchers, and Other Folklore Tales of Westmeath*, by Patrick Bardan, Westmeath Guardian Office, 1891; and *Fairy and Folk Tales of the Irish Peasantry*, Edited and Selected by W.B. Yeats, Walker Scott, 1888.

And a very special and heartfelt thank you to my wife, Marilyn. Being married to a writer, she lives with the stories I tell as much as I do. As my first reader, she offers her support and advice. I'm thankful every day for her love, understanding, patience, and humor.

Thomas D. Clagett
Santa Fe, New Mexico

# About the Author

Award winning author Thomas D. Clagett has always had a passion for the American West, for film and for writing. His novels include the Gothic Western, *Blood West*, *Line of Glory: a Novel of the Alamo*, and *West of Penance*. A lover of film, he is also the author of *William Friedkin: Films of Aberration, Obsession and Reality*. Find out more at www.thomasdclagett.com.